THE
FURTHER ADVENTURES
OF
PERIWINKLE
PIG

THE
FURTHER ADVENTURES
OF
PERIWINKLE
PIG

By Peter Cutler and Kath Kyle

Matador
Unit E2 Airfield Business Park,
Harrison Road, Market Harborough,
Leicestershire. LE16 7UL
Tel: 0116 2792299
Email: books@troubador.co.uk
Web: www.troubador.co.uk/matador
Twitter: @matadorbooks

ISBN 978 1803135 168

British Library Cataloguing in Publication Data.
A catalogue record for this book is available from the British Library.

Printed and bound in Great Britain by 4edge Limited
Typeset in 12pt Minion Pro by Troubador Publishing Ltd, Leicester, UK

Matador is an imprint of Troubador Publishing Ltd

For Matt who has always encouraged
and believed in me.

CONTENTS

A piglet continues
his journey to discover the world.

PERIWINKLE PIG AND THE CITY

Periwinkle arrives in France

Ever since he had been a very little piglet Periwinkle Pig had been fascinated by maps and by pictures of far-away places. He loved to read about great explorers who had caught boats and walked through jungles and discovered places that nobody had even known were there. He dreamed that one day he too might find somewhere new and, when he left school, he set off to make his dream come true.

He had planned his journey carefully and decided that he would start by travelling to Egypt. He thought it looked like an absolutely fascinating place and it was, he was sure, very close to places that hadn't yet been found.

His mother had made him a seemingly never-ending supply of sandwiches and he had packed those into a duffel bag. He had collected together all manner of things that he was sure would be useful for an exploring piglet; elastic bands, pieces of string, some spare socks, a slightly rusty penknife that his Uncle Peter had given him and, most importantly, a little compass that very cleverly always pointed North, no matter how often you turned it around and tried to make it dizzy.

After hugging his mother and waving goodbye to his family and friends he had set off from home and made his way to the south coast of England. He knew that was where he needed to go first in order to cross the English Channel which is the place where England finishes and the rest of the world begins.

A few times he had been given a lift in a motor car which helped him to make progress quickly but for most of the time he had walked. Along the way he had met a variety of people and other creatures and he had had some quite splendid adventures. He was pleased that he had become an explorer.

At the south coast he had met a warm-hearted couple, Mr and Mrs Baldwin, who had agreed to take him with them to France in their boat.

He didn't really like the way that the sea made the boat bob around. It went up and down and from side to side. It made his head spin and his tummy didn't feel quite right. But he enjoyed talking to Mr and

Mrs Baldwin and occasionally he had a nibble of a sandwich or biscuit to see if that made him feel any better.

After a few hours on the boat Periwinkle began to see a thin line of green sandwiched between the dark blue of the sea and the paler blue of the sky. As they sailed towards it the line got thicker and thicker and, just as he was starting to realise what he was seeing, "There you are Periwinkle," announced Mr Baldwin. "That's France! Looks all sort of French doesn't it?"

To Periwinkle it just looked like a green stripe but he happily agreed with Mr Baldwin that it did look sort of French.

"Goodness me!" he exclaimed. "France. Golly gosh. Just waiting for me to arrive and have more adventures. Mind you," he went on thoughtfully, "I'm still a long way from Egypt aren't I?"

"Why yes, young Periwinkle," agreed Mr Baldwin. "Egypt is still an awfully long way. But there will be lots for you to see and explore on your way there."

Not too much later Mr Baldwin stopped the boat next to a sort of wooden path and jumped out onto the path. He tied a rope from the boat to a post that was conveniently sticking up close by and then he and Mrs Baldwin helped Periwinkle off the boat. He needed help because his legs seemed to have stopped working properly. He'd noticed before that bobbing around in a boat had that effect and he idly wondered why Mr and Mrs Baldwin didn't seem to be having the same problem. Maybe it was just something that affected piglets he wondered.

"This is where we leave you to your travels." Mr Baldwin held out his hand to shake hands with Periwinkle.

"Take care young pigling," added Mrs Baldwin as she planted a kiss on the top of Periwinkle's head which would have made him blush a deep pink if he hadn't already been a very pink piglet.

With their 'goodbyes' and 'good-lucks' ringing in his ears, Periwinkle walked unsteadily along the wooden path until he came to a road. He took a deep breath, set his nose resolutely in front of him and stepped out onto the road. His first steps on French soil.

"I'm here! I'm in France! I'm abroad!" Periwinkle did a little dance of joy although, as his legs still felt strange, it was an odd little dance. He decided that he should maybe leave dancing until he felt a bit more like himself.

He looked to the left and to the right. The road went in both directions as roads have a tendency to do.

"But which way is Egypt?" he puzzled. It had been very simple journeying in England because he knew that he just had to keep going south and would eventually end up at the coast. It wasn't so simple here and there were no friendly road signs telling him which way to go as there had been on the English lanes.

He tried to picture his maps. He wasn't sure which bit of France he was in because he knew that France had a lot of coast. But he was almost totally certain that, on his maps, Egypt was to the right of France and further down the page. That meant that he had to travel sort of south and east … if only he could work out which way that was from where he was now.

So, for the first time in this part of his adventures, Periwinkle reached into his duffel bag and pulled out his compass. It was such a clever gadget that, even though he was no longer in England, Periwinkle knew that it would still faithfully point to the north and so he would be able to work out which way he needed to travel. He turned it around a few times, checked it carefully and then, following its instructions, he set off determinedly along the road in what he was confident was the right direction.

He hadn't walked very far before he realised that after such a busy day and a long sea journey he was feeling tired so he decided to look for somewhere to spend the night.

To be honest he wasn't in a great hurry to get anywhere at all. He still very much wanted to get to Egypt but he was happy to spend some time exploring Europe on his way.

"After all, I can discover things anywhere I go and there might even be places in Europe that people haven't discovered yet. So yes, I have the whole of

Europe to start exploring and it's always better to do things like that after a decent night's sleep."

Fortunately, he only had to walk a short way further before he came to a hedge which looked as though it would provide a comfortable shelter for the night.

He sat down. He nibbled another sandwich. His tummy was starting to feel much better and he realised that he was actually rather hungry.

As the sun disappeared under the blanket of the sky and the moon took its place to provide some light Periwinkle lay down with a smile on his face. He reflected on the events of the day and the adventures that were surely to come and before long he fell into a very deep and very happy sleep.

Periwinkle sees the sights

The next day dawned bright and clear. Periwinkle refreshed himself with a few acorns that he found conveniently under a tree not far from where he had slept overnight. He was pleased to discover that there were acorns in France.

After checking his compass to make sure he was still heading sort of south and east Periwinkle set off to begin his wandering through France.

He had to keep reminding himself that he was in France because, truth to tell, he didn't think it looked much different to some of the places he had wandered through in England. The country lanes still looked like country lanes. The fields were the same shade of green. There were daisies and buttercups underneath the hedges and the trees were like English trees.

But, even if it didn't look much different, it all looked very splendid and colourful with the sun shining down as he walked.

He passed all manner of creatures who sat underneath the hedges. He called a cheery "Bonjour!" to the birds in the trees and the sheep in the fields, feeling very French as he did it because he knew that "Bonjour" is what the French say instead of "Hello". "Bonjour little pigling!" they called back to him and the birds twittered a few other things too but Periwinkle couldn't understand what they were saying. He knew they were being friendly though so he waved at them as he passed.

He walked through villages where the shops called themselves things like 'Boulangerie' which, on closer inspection, Periwinkle found to sell nothing but bread and 'Fromagerie' which sold nothing but cheese and was just a little bit smelly to Periwinkle's way of thinking.

Outside some shops were tables piled high with fruit and vegetables. There were curvy green cucumbers; watermelons so huge that Periwinkle was sure they would be too heavy for one person to lift on their own; bright orange apricots and peaches; and cherries that were such a dark red that they looked almost black. Everything looked very fresh as though it had just been picked from out of the nearby fields.

On the roads and in the villages there were men on bicycles and little motor scooters which made a sort of popping noise, and they were all zooming dangerously along so that, quite often, Periwinkle had to jump back onto the grass at the side of the road to get out of their way.

After a lot of walking he saw a signpost which suggested that he wasn't far from somewhere famous.

"Paris!" he grinned. "I've walked to Paris!"

He knew that Paris was a very large city and he'd never been to a large city before. To be honest he'd never wanted to. He was quite content with country lanes and villages and found that they provided all the excitement and adventures that he wanted. But, on the other hand, this was Paris. In France. It had lots of famous buildings and Periwinkle thought he really ought to take the opportunity to see some of them.

As he walked on, the buildings got closer together and there were more people and it was all very busy and noisy. There were cars and motorbikes vrooming around and the sounds of horns being blown and people shouting. There was more traffic than he had ever seen in one place and Periwinkle wasn't sure that he liked it very much. He didn't think he would stay in Paris very long. Just long enough to see the things he wanted to see.

He walked around, trying his best to avoid being run over by the cars and the motorbikes. He saw a very big church. Then another even bigger church which looked very different to the first one. He saw an old building that a sign told him was a museum and then another that was an art gallery.

He stood for a while to watch some boats on the river. He waved to the people who were travelling on the boats and they waved back to him.

There were lots of statues: Statues of people standing and looking into the distance. Statues of horses. Statues of people on horses. He noticed that there weren't any statues of pigs.

"Maybe one day, when I'm a famous explorer," he chuckled to himself, "Someone will make a statue of me. Periwinkle Pig, Explorer."

The other thing he noticed about the statues was that there were pigeons sitting on all of them. Not statues of pigeons. Real pigeons. Occasionally one of them took off, flew around a little and then landed on the statue again. He watched, fascinated by this strange behaviour. After a few minutes one of the pigeons landed right next to where he was standing. It was a plump grey bird. The feathers on its chest were white and those on the back of its small but very round head were a metallic green colour that shone in the Paris sunshine.

"Hello little piglet," said the pigeon. "I'm Percy. Who might you be and what is a piglet doing in the centre of Paris? We don't get many piglets here as a rule."

Periwinkle introduced himself.

"I am Periwinkle Pig, Explorer. I have travelled from England and I am on my way to Egypt and from there to discover places that haven't been discovered before. I am hoping to explore a few places on my way to Egypt and to have some adventures. I had lots of adventures before I even left England."

He asked Percy the question that had come to his mind when he was looking at the statues.

"Tell me Percy. Why does every statue have a pigeon sitting on it?"

Percy gave him a quizzical look.

"When did you ever see a statue without a pigeon on it? It's our hobby."

He explained that pigeons wait until tourists are about to take a photograph of a statue and then they go to sit on it.

"The men and women wave their little arms around and they stamp their feet and they shout things like 'shoo!' and overall they look very silly. Sometimes I take off and fly around for a bit and then, just as they think I've gone and they hold their cameras up, I land back again. It drives them crazy! Such fun we have!"

Periwinkle had never heard of such a hobby. He understood hobbies to be about collecting stamps like his Uncle Peter or knitting blankets like his Auntie

Pauline. He didn't think it was very kind to find fun by annoying people.

"I'm in thousands and thousands of photos," Percy continued and Periwinkle began to suspect that the pigeon was just a bit of a show-off.

"And now if you'll excuse me Periwinkle Pig, there's a statue over there with no pigeon on it at all." Percy flew off and landed on a statue of a man who looked very important. A lady who was about to take a photograph of the statue waved her arms around, just as Percy had described.

A thought occurred to Periwinkle. He wondered whether pigeons were related to pigs. He'd never heard that they were but, if they weren't, then why did their name start with the word 'pig'? Perhaps, he wondered, they might be the flying branch of the family. It was one of those questions that he really wanted to know the answer to but right at that moment he wasn't sure how he could find out. He made a note in his head to look it up in his books when he got back home. Whenever that might be.

He shook his head and brought himself back to thinking about where he was rather than about questions that he didn't know the answer to. He was here … in Paris … in France … and there was more exploring to be done so he walked on.

Periwinkle climbs a tower

To Periwinkle's way of thinking Paris was a bit too big and a lot too noisy and he was looking forward to returning to the peace and quiet of the country lanes. But, first, there was one thing that he very much wanted to see.

He walked on and once or twice he stopped to ask a passer-by for directions. At last he turned a corner and there it was.

"The Eiffel Tower!" he beamed. "The most famous place in the whole of France." He had seen pictures of it but he hadn't realised how tall it was. Living up to its name, it towered up into the sky, pointing at the clouds like a huge arrow. It seemed to stretch upwards for ever. It was the tallest thing that Periwinkle had ever seen.

He could see people at the top of the tower, looking very small because they were so high up. It would surely be a fine adventure to go to the top but Periwinkle didn't much like the idea of climbing up all the steps to get there. It would be hard on his little legs and take far too long. Maybe it would be better, now that he'd seen it, just to find his way out of Paris and continue his journeying.

As he began to walk away he noticed that on one of the corners of the tower was a doorway and a sign over that doorway said 'Lift'. Periwinkle knew that a lift was a sort of metal box which people got into and which was attached to a metal rope which pulled it up and let it back down. He thought about it and realised that he, Periwinkle, could get in a lift and go to the top of this amazing tower. He wouldn't have to climb up lots of steps and it surely wouldn't take too long at all.

He was very tempted but he expected it would cost a lot of money. He only had six pennies in his duffel bag and he might need those later in his travels so he shouldn't spend them to go up a tower, however famous it was and however impressive it looked.

It wouldn't hurt to find out though, just to be sure.

"Excuse me sir," he addressed a man in a uniform who was standing next to the doorway. "How much would it cost to go in the lift to the top of this wonderful tower … and to come back down again of course," he added, just in case it wasn't clear that that was what he meant.

"Free today. Always free on the first of the month."

That was interesting news. Periwinkle hadn't even known that it was the first of the month. He thought about it again and decided to delay his onward journeying for a little while longer. Besides which he had never actually been in a lift before so that would be a new adventure for him anyway.

He walked through the doorway and got into a lift which began its journey upwards. He was slightly alarmed to find his tummy feeling a bit strange. Not strange like it had been on the boat to France but just … strange. He gulped a bit and hoped that it was a very strong rope that was holding the lift. But of course it was. Lifts are always attached to very strong ropes.

Before too long the lift doors opened again and Periwinkle stepped out. Oh my goodness! He was ever so high above the ground. He looked down, holding very tightly onto a railing that was all that seemed to be stopping him falling right off the side of the tower.

Down below he could see mile after mile of buildings and roads and traffic all whizzing around, looking like tiny ants from this distance. He could just make out the two big churches that he'd seen earlier. They looked very small.

A silver band wound its way between the buildings and Periwinkle realised that was the river. By looking very hard he could make out some boats like the ones that he had stood to watch.

"How did you get up here?"

Periwinkle turned round to see where the voice had come from. There was a pigeon sitting on the railing. It didn't look like a very safe thing to do but, of course, if the pigeon fell off then he could just flap his wings and fly so he wouldn't fall to the ground. Unlike piglets who really shouldn't sit on railings at the top of tall towers.

The pigeon was grey with a green head and a white chest. It looked like Percy the pigeon but Periwinkle thought that one pigeon probably looked much like another. Unlike pigs of course who all look very different to each other.

"Not speaking to me Periwinkle?" the pigeon asked. It was Percy!

"Ha ha, I didn't recognise you for a moment there," Periwinkle confessed.

"Didn't recognise me? What a bad memory you must have. Not sure how you're going to get to Egypt if you can't even remember a pigeon you met not half an hour ago. In fact, I'm surprised you can even remember where it is you're trying to get to!"

Periwinkle was going to explain that he thought all pigeons looked the same but then he realised that might sound rude so he left the thought inside his head which is where such thoughts should remain.

"What a great view you get from up here," he commented instead.

"It's not as good as the view I get when I'm flying around but it's the best you'll see, what with you being a piglet and not a bird."

Something about what Percy said reminded Periwinkle of a thought he'd had earlier but he couldn't quite remember what it was.

"You didn't answer my question anyway. How did you get up here, what with you being a piglet?" asked Percy again.

"Explorers can do that sort of thing," replied Periwinkle rather vaguely. He felt a bit bad at not telling Percy about the lift and about it being free on the first of the month but he didn't think Percy would understand about lifts. Pigeons don't need lifts, they just flap their wings very hard if they want to go upwards.

In any case Periwinkle was starting to think that he had had enough of looking down at the view. Fascinating though it was it was getting late in the afternoon and he really needed to make his way out of Paris and find somewhere to spend the night.

"I've enjoyed meeting you Percy," he went on. "And this has been an interesting adventure but now I am going to go back to the ground so that I can continue my travels."

"OK Periwinkle, I'll leave you to it. I'd better get back to my statues anyway. Best of luck for your journey." And with that the pigeon flew away into the distance and Periwinkle stepped back into the lift.

Going downwards made Periwinkle's tummy feel even stranger than it had done on the way up. Back on the ground he had one of his biscuits to make himself feel better, then checked his compass and set off to resume his journeying in a sort of south and east direction towards Egypt.

He walked until he got to a place where he could no longer hear the traffic and see the lights and smell the smells of Paris. He was glad to have seen such a famous place but he had found it a most exhausting experience. The countryside felt more gentle. It was more colourful. He could hear the chitter chatter of the birds and the gentle mooing of the cows and even the excited scampering of the rabbits in the fields that he passed.

He settled down for the night in some comfortable looking leaves next to a small stream.

Just as he was dropping off to sleep he remembered what it was that had bothered him about his last conversation with Percy the pigeon. He had completely forgotten to ask him if he knew whether pigeons were related to pigs.

"Oh well," he said to himself sleepily. "I think that's a question for another day." And with that he fell into a contented sleep.

Periwinkle gets covered in paint

Periwinkle woke the next morning, stretched his arms, took some deep breaths of the clean country air, nibbled a sandwich and drank some water. He checked his compass and set off again, looking forward to the day ahead.

The morning passed without adventure but Periwinkle was just pleased to walk along the lanes, back in the peace and quiet of the countryside.

During the afternoon he came to a gate. A head was peering over the top. It had long ears that pointed upwards from either side of a soft brown face. Periwinkle was fairly sure it was a donkey. He had always found donkeys to be quiet and sometimes miserable so he was pleased to see a smile on the face of this one.

"Hello little pigling," said the donkey. "Don't see many piglings along here. Don't see many people either. Are you staying long? It's nice to have company for a change."

Periwinkle had only intended to say hello as he passed but he was a kind little piglet and decided to keep the donkey company for a while.

"I'm pleased to meet you Donkey. I can't stay for too long though. I am an explorer and I am on my way to Egypt."

"Egypt eh?" said the donkey. "Is that nearby?"

Periwinkle was going to laugh but then he remembered that not everybody had read as many books about the world as he had read so they might not know where Egypt was.

"Oh no Donkey. It's a long way away from here."

"You'd better not stop to talk to me then. You'll have to get on your way if you're going to get there today."

Periwinkle explained that he wasn't going to get there today. In fact, he might not get there for quite a lot of weeks.

"I'm just exploring around here today. Are there any interesting places for me to visit?"

"I don't know," replied the donkey. "I've never been out of this field."

That shocked Periwinkle.

"The gate doesn't open," went on the donkey. "So I can't get out. Rabbits jump in and out through the gaps in the gate. Mice walk underneath it. There was a horse in here with me once and she jumped right over it. I tried that but it didn't go too well. I was very sore afterwards and I didn't get out anyway."

Periwinkle looked at the gate. He couldn't see a lock on the outside of it. He tried to look over the top but there didn't appear to be a lock on the inside of it either. So why, he wondered, wouldn't the gate open? As he was climbing back down from peering over the top of it he saw a piece of rope which looped around the gatepost. He lifted it up, pulled the gate and, to the donkey's amazement, it swung open.

"You're a magician as well as an explorer. How did you do that?"

Periwinkle closed the gate, put the rope back over it, pulled the gate and, of course, it didn't open.

"I'm stuck again!" cried the donkey.

Periwinkle lifted the rope, pulled the gate and it opened again. He showed the donkey how it worked and suggested that he tried it for himself.

"That's amazing. Now I can come for a walk with you. I don't think I'll walk as far as Egypt though. Not if it's a very long way."

Periwinkle and the donkey walked along the lane and as they walked they talked. Well, in truth, it was Periwinkle that did most of the talking. The donkey had never been out of the field and therefore his stories were all a bit the same.

A thought struck Periwinkle and, passing quickly from his brain to his mouth, it burst out through his lips.

"You've never told me your name!"

"I don't have one," replied the donkey.

"You must have a name! Everybody's got a name."

"No. I don't have a name. People just call me Donkey."

That struck Periwinkle as very sad. He might have been given the wrong name because of the man in the office who'd been rather old and very deaf, but at least he'd got a name.

"Well, I'm going to call you Daniel," he announced. "I think that's an excellent name for a donkey."

The donkey thought about it for a moment.

"Daniel the donkey," he repeated a few times as though trying it for size. "Daniel the donkey. Yes, I like that. I'm Daniel the donkey and I'm no longer stuck in that field. How pleased I am that you came along today Periwinkle."

And Periwinkle smiled because he always liked to make people happy.

Before too long the pair came to a busy little village.

In the village was a pretty square with a fountain and flower beds and a café with chairs and tables outside. People were sitting drinking coffee and eating cake that looked tasty and reminded Periwinkle that it was nearly time for a biscuit.

One of the ladies sitting outside the café placed her handbag on the ground next to her. In a flash a man appeared from nowhere, lifted it off the ground and walked away very quickly.

Periwinkle could hardly believe what he'd seen. He only knew that he had to get the lady's handbag back.

"Stop!" he shouted. "Stop, thief!"

Daniel the donkey shouted the same although it came out more as a sort of "Brayyyyy!" noise as that's how donkeys talk when they're agitated.

The thief began to run. Now pigs aren't as fast at running as horses or goats but they're not as slow as cows or hedgehogs and Periwinkle had even won a prize at school for running. He'd got a little medal for it. So he ran. So too did Daniel the donkey and also the lady who now realised that her handbag had been stolen.

Running through the village they dodged around people, pushchairs, motor scooters and the like.

The thief knocked into a ladder and a man who had been at the top of the ladder painting a window dropped his can of paint in alarm. It went flying right up into the air and a lot of the paint landed on Periwinkle! But that didn't stop him running.

Eventually he was near enough to throw himself forward and grab hold of the thief's legs to bring him crashing to the ground. Daniel the donkey jumped onto the scoundrel's back to hold him down. The lady whose bag had been stolen grabbed it back from the thief who scampered away once Daniel stepped off him.

"What a brave piglet you are!" exclaimed the lady very gratefully and then, noticing that Periwinkle was covered in paint, she invited him to go home with her. "I will wash your clothes and give you some warm water and soap to get rid of all that paint and restore your lovely pink colour. And then perhaps you would like to sleep in my barn overnight?"

Periwinkle was happy to accept the offer as he hadn't been sure where he was going to spend the night. He said goodbye to Daniel the donkey who had decided to head back to his field and turn in for the night. "I've enjoyed my day out with you Periwinkle and it's been very exciting. Now that you've shown me how to open the gate I can have a walk any time I want. Good luck for Egypt and all that."

Periwinkle went with the lady back to her house. Freshly washed and with newly laundered clothes he made himself comfortable in her barn, ate some supper that she brought out for him and then settled himself down to sleep after yet another day of adventures.

PERIWINKLE PIG AND
THE HARVEST

Periwinkle rides a bicycle

Periwinkle Pig had left his home in England to explore the world and, he hoped, find places that hadn't yet been discovered. He was heading first to Egypt and had already got as far as France. He knew that he still had a long way to travel but that didn't worry him. He kept finding, as he had in England, that it wasn't difficult for an exploring piglet to find adventures wherever he was.

One morning he awoke after a good night's sleep in a barn. Well, to be exact, his brain woke up and then waited a few moments for his body to catch up with it. It was strange the way that happened, he thought. Some days his body woke up first and it took a while for his brain to catch up. But not today. Today his brain was wide awake and it took a little while before his fingers and toes were happy to be wiggled out of their comfortable sleep.

"Come on Periwinkle," he told himself. "It's time to be getting on with the journey."

After a few acorns and a drink of water, he was ready to go. He took his little compass out of his duffel bag and, as always, it very cleverly pointed towards north. That meant he knew which way he had to go to continue his journeying sort of south and east which was the right direction to go to get to Egypt.

As he walked along the country lanes and through the villages he noticed that a lot of people were riding along on bicycles. Big bicycles, little ones, red ones, green ones, shiny ones and rusty ones. Ones with big handlebars that stuck right up into the air and ones with little handlebars that looked only just big enough for the rider to hold onto. Some people cycled along in a jolly manner and called and waved to him as they passed. Others had their heads down and their legs were pedalling very hard and they looked as though they were trying to get somewhere very quickly.

Occasionally he saw someone carrying boxes or bales of hay on their bicycle and that made them wobble around in a way that Periwinkle didn't think looked at all safe.

Most of the people riding the bicycles looked very happy although sometimes a car would come along going fast and, when that happened, the rider would wave a fist into the air and shout something that didn't sound very friendly at all.

It all made Periwinkle think about whether he might be able to cycle for some of his journey. He wasn't sure that he had enough money to buy a bicycle which might be a problem but it was certainly something that he should investigate.

Now, in one of those strange coincidences that only ever happen in books and in films, just as he was thinking about this he turned round a bend in the lane and there was a bicycle leaning against a wall! It wasn't a very shiny bicycle but it had two wheels and some handlebars and a saddle which is a sort of seat that bicycles have.

Periwinkle stopped in his tracks.

"How very strange," he laughed. "There was I thinking about where I might get a bicycle and now there's one right in front of me!"

He shook his head.

"But, of course, this isn't my bicycle and they don't just appear out of nowhere so it must belong to somebody."

He looked all around him. He looked forwards and backwards and sideways and upwards and downwards. There wasn't anyone within sight.

"Hmmm," he sighed.

He knew he couldn't just take the bicycle. It wasn't his so that would be stealing which is a very bad thing to do. But he did very much like the idea of having a ride on it. He'd never ridden one before and, if he was going to travel part of the way to Egypt on one, then it was perhaps sensible to see what it was like. Maybe he could just ride a few yards down the lane and then turn around and come back again and leave the bicycle just where he had found it. Yes, that was a good plan.

He carefully wheeled the bicycle onto the lane. He put one leg across it onto one of the pedals and tried to pull himself up onto the seat. That wasn't too easy. He tried and he tried and, every time, he wobbled around a bit and didn't reach the seat. This was an unexpected setback.

He took a deep breath and tried again. This time he was almost sure he was going to do it but, at the last moment, it was all a bit too far out of reach and he wobbled a bit too much and the bicycle wobbled a bit too much too. Before he knew what had happened, he was on the ground with the bicycle on top of him.

"Ouch," he cried, for it is painful to fall off a bicycle, particularly when that bicycle falls on top of you.

"What's happening?!" came a voice from behind the wall where the bicycle had been leaning. "And what is a pigling doing underneath my bicycle?" it added.

Although he had looked around to try to find the owner of the bicycle, Periwinkle had failed to notice a red-faced gentleman who appeared to have been having a little sleep at the other side of the wall.

Periwinkle was very apologetic and explained that he hadn't been intending to steal the bicycle but he was on his way to Egypt and was thinking about cycling some of the way so had just wanted to give it a try.

"I've never been on a bicycle before you see. I was only going to go a few yards but I couldn't even get onto the seat," he finished a bit sadly.

By this time the man with the red face had come out of the field and was trying to help disentangle Periwinkle from the bicycle.

"A pig on a bicycle!" he laughed. "Well why not? And yes, it seems sensible to try it if you're going to cycle all the way to Egypt. Let me lift you onto the saddle and I'll push you off down the lane."

That seemed a very kind offer so Periwinkle smiled back and said thank you very much. He held onto the handlebars and the man with the red face lifted him onto the seat and held the bicycle until it stopped wobbling and then pushed Periwinkle off down the lane.

It was at this point that Periwinkle discovered another sad fact. Piglets aren't really the right shape for bicycles. They have shorter legs than human persons and when Periwinkle was sitting on the seat and holding onto the handlebars he couldn't actually reach the pedals.

"Help!" he shouted and the man with the red face, realising what was happening, came dashing along and grabbed hold of him just before Periwinkle and the bicycle were about to go crashing back to the ground. Periwinkle jumped off the seat and landed on the ground very shakily.

"It seems to me young pigling," said the man with the red face, "that you might need to rethink your plan to cycle to Egypt. You're not really made for a bicycle are you?"

Periwinkle agreed that he wasn't really made for a bicycle.

"But thank you sir for letting me try. It is another adventure that I have had and I am grateful to you for that. But perhaps now I should carry on walking."

With that he dusted himself down, shook hands with the man with the red face and set off on his travels again with no more thoughts about cycling to Egypt.

Periwinkle hears about a forgetful farmer

After taking his leave of the man with the red face and the bicycle Periwinkle continued to walk along the lane.

He came to a field in which two young goats were playing. They were chasing each other round and round, occasionally bumping their heads together. Sometimes their feet went a bit too fast for their bodies and they tumbled head over heels. They didn't appear to hurt themselves though. They just picked themselves up and kept on playing.

Periwinkle stood by the gate of the field to watch them, amused by their antics. Suddenly they spotted him and dashed over to say hello. They dashed so quickly that they couldn't stop in time and hit the gate with a bump. Periwinkle jumped backwards as their heads came straight through the gap between the planks of wood that formed the gate. He wasn't sure how they had even managed to get their heads through the gap as they both had horns on the top of their heads

"I say, don't get your heads stuck in there will you?" he warned.

"No, not at all. We do this all the time," replied the larger of the two.

They nodded their heads up and down and Periwinkle thought that they were most unlikely to be able to get out of the gap in the gate but they seemed happy enough and insisted that they weren't stuck so he moved on to other things.

"I am Periwinkle Pig," he introduced himself.

The larger of the two goats said that his name was Gordon and the other goat was his sister Gail.

"I'm pleased to meet you Gordon and Gail. I am an explorer and I have travelled from England. I am on my way to Egypt but, at the moment, I am exploring France."

"An explorer? Hmm, you'll have something to eat in that bag of yours then," stated Gordon hopefully. "You can't be going to do much exploring without having something to eat in your bag."

"Oh please say you've got something to eat," added Gail. "Piglets always have something to eat in their bags. We're ever so hungry."

The goats went on to explain that the farmer who looked after them had forgotten to give them any breakfast that morning.

"He'll have slept in again."

"Probably had too much wine last night."

"He's always having too much wine."

"And then he sleeps in."

"He forgets us."

"And we haven't had any breakfast!" they both finished together.

Periwinkle looked past them into the field. "But don't goats eat grass?" he asked, rather confused. "And it seems to me there's an awful lot of grass in that field you're in. Why can't you eat that?"

"Grass?" Gordon sneered in a way that implied that Periwinkle had said something nasty. "Grass? You think we should eat grass do you? Have you ever tried eating grass?"

Periwinkle admitted that he hadn't actually tried eating grass. Walked on it. Sat on it. Slept on it. But never actually eaten it.

"Exactly. So why do you think we should eat it?"

"Because you're goats?" suggested Periwinkle helplessly.

"Yes of course we eat grass!" said Gordon, leaving Periwinkle feeling more confused than ever. "But not all the time. Not for breakfast. Not for lunch. And definitely, definitely not for dinner. Grass is more like … well I suppose you might call it a snack."

Now, Periwinkle still had some sandwiches and some biscuits in his duffel bag. He had been hoping that they would last him for most of his journeying so he was a bit reluctant to give any away. But, on the other hand, he was a kind little piglet and it felt very sad that the farmer kept forgetting to feed the goats. He reached into his duffel bag and pulled out a couple of biscuits. They were grabbed very quickly and, before Periwinkle could even notice it happening, had disappeared into the goats' mouths.

"Mmmmm … don't shupposhe you … nnn … chomp chomp … switch do you?" spluttered Gordon with his mouth still full of biscuit. It made it a bit difficult to understand what he was saying.

"Nice cheese san… switch … chomp chomp …" contributed Gail and Periwinkle got the general idea.

"No cheese," he informed them, totally truthfully. "But I could spare you a peanut butter sandwich if that would do?"

The goats looked at each other and agreed that a peanut butter sandwich would do nicely.

Periwinkle handed over a couple of peanut butter sandwiches. The sight of his sandwiches reminded him that he too was a bit hungry, it being a long time since he had breakfasted on a few acorns.

"I think I will take a break from my journeying and join you in a sandwich," and he settled himself down on a patch of grass at the side of the gate.

"So tell me about your farmer," he invited. "And why you continue to stay with someone who forgets to feed you."

There was no answer and Periwinkle thought at first that the goats hadn't heard him but then he realised that they were too busy eating the sandwiches. A soft munching noise continued for a few moments and then, eventually, with a gulp and a lick of his lips, Gordon began to tell their story.

"You see Periwinkle, it's like this. The farmer's name is Mr Labouche. Many years ago he grew potatoes and corn and vegetables. He had a few ducks and some hens and he was just an ordinary sort of farmer. One day he bought another field and he planted it with grape trees and now he grows enough grapes to be able to make his own wine. He sells some of it but it is such lovely wine that he can't resist drinking it. Then it makes him sleep and when he wakes up he has a headache and he can't think about very much so he forgets to come to feed us.

"But he's not a bad man really and he always

remembers us in the end. In fact, that's his tractor coming down the lane now."

Periwinkle looked down the lane and, sure enough, there was a rather dirty and rusty green tractor heading towards them.

"He'll be coming to give us our lunch" cheered Gail very happily and Periwinkle began to think that he hadn't needed to share his sandwiches with the goats after all.

Mr Labouche climbed down from his tractor and looked at the goats. "I see you've got your heads caught in the gate again. And who is this piglet that you're talking to?"

Periwinkle introduced himself and explained that he was an explorer on his way to Egypt and that he was having adventures along the way. Talking about that reminded him that he wasn't having much in the way of new adventures whilst he was standing here talking to a forgetful farmer and a couple of goats with their heads stuck in a gate.

He stood up.

"Well, much as I have enjoyed speaking to you it is time that I moved on to find new adventures and get closer to Egypt. Goodbye Gordon. Goodbye Gail. Goodbye Farmer Labouche."

He checked his compass, put it back into his duffel bag and, with a wave to the farmer and the goats, he continued on his way.

Periwinkle helps with the harvest

After meeting the goats and the forgetful farmer Periwinkle continued his journey in a sort of south and east direction. A few days later, on a bright and sunny morning, he was walking along a lane where there were few hedges and he noticed that the fields at the side of the lane looked to have dark green stripes across them which stretched on and on as far as Periwinkle could see. He thought he would take a few moments out of his journeying to inspect the scene more closely.

After looking for a while he realised that the stripes were actually rows of plants. On even further inspection he could see that there were people in the fields, walking between the stripes and carrying baskets. There were lots of people. They were brightly dressed and calling to one another and they all looked to be having a splendid time. He had a feeling he knew what they were doing and he thought he might walk into the field to talk to them so that he could be sure.

"Enjoying the scenery are you? It's quite a sight isn't it?"

Periwinkle had been so fascinated by what was going on in the field that he hadn't even noticed a farmer come along on a blue tractor that was much shinier than the one that Farmer Labouche had driven.

He agreed with the farmer that it certainly was quite a sight. "Tell me sir," he started. "Are those grape trees in the fields?"

The farmer laughed. "I suppose you could call them grape trees. They're actually called vines. They're a very special sort of tree."

"And are those people in the field picking the grapes?" Periwinkle prodded.

The farmer confirmed that the people in the field were picking the grapes. "It's harvest time you see. The grapes are perfect now and we have to finish picking them today otherwise they'll be no good for making wine."

He explained that many of his neighbours had come to help and that, when their own grapes were ready for picking, he would go to help them. Periwinkle thought it was wonderful that they all helped each other like that.

"We can always do with an extra pair of hands," added the farmer. "I can't afford to pay you but I can give you some refreshments if you'd like to join us?"

Periwinkle happily agreed to help and it was only a little bit to do with the mention of refreshments. Picking grapes was another fine adventure for him to have. He'd never picked grapes before. Potatoes often and even sometimes cabbages but never grapes. They hadn't grown grapes where he lived in England and he didn't think there would be any opportunity to pick grapes once he got to Egypt.

"Jump on the tractor then and I'll take you up to the field and get you started."

The farmer leaned down and gave Periwinkle a hand to climb up on the tractor and, once Periwinkle was sitting on the seat behind the farmer, the tractor set off towards the fields.

"Goodness, this is going to be a day of adventures," thought Periwinkle. "I've never ridden on a tractor before and now I'm going to pick grapes which I've also never done before. How happy I am to be an explorer!" He only realised that he had spoken those last few words out loud when the farmer looked over his shoulder at him.

"You're an explorer? A piglet who is an explorer?"

So Periwinkle introduced himself and explained that he was an exploring piglet who was on his way to see things and discover places that haven't been discovered before.

"I am on my way to Egypt which I know has already been discovered but it sounds like an absolutely fascinating place and I'm sure it must be very close to places that nobody has found before."

"I'm pleased to make your acquaintance Periwinkle," said the farmer who introduced himself as Mr Charpentier.

The tractor took them far into the field and, after jumping off the seat that he'd ridden on, Periwinkle set to work. He wasn't entirely sure what to do but he watched what other people were doing and it didn't seem too difficult. Now that he was closer to the grape trees he could see that, hanging from them, were lots and lots of bunches of plump purple grapes. They were so fat that they looked as though they were going to burst out of their skins. Periwinkle realised that he was expected to pull the bunches from the grape trees and put them into a basket that he'd been given to carry.

Every now and again Mr Charpentier drove along and tipped the grapes out of Periwinkle's basket into another enormous basket that he was pulling along behind his tractor.

Some of the people who were picking the grapes were singing. A man was playing a guitar. From time to time a few people would put down their baskets and dance. It was almost like a party.

The sun was shining and it was very hot. Occasionally when Periwinkle thought nobody was looking he popped one of the grapes into his mouth, savouring its sweetness and its refreshing juiciness. He guessed these grapes would make very good wine. Not that he knew what good wine tasted like of course. Or any wine for that matter.

Periwinkle didn't know how long he'd been picking grapes but after a while the other people who were picking the grapes put down their baskets.

"Come on little pigling," they called to him. "Time to eat."

That sounded most agreeable to Periwinkle so he followed them to a large tent that had been set up further along the field. Inside the tent were long wooden tables which had been piled high with food. He took a seat with the other grape pickers and studied what looked to be a marvellous feast.

There was bread that, when he picked it up, felt warm as though it had just been baked.

There were salad leaves that were bright green and curly and tomatoes that were red and shiny.

There was cheese. Lots of different types of it. Periwinkle was beginning to realise that no meal in France was felt to be complete without a great deal of cheese.

There were lots of other types of food on the table. Periwinkle tried it all and, if there were a few things that he wasn't too keen on, he found that most of it was absolutely delicious.

On the table were jugs filled with cold water which was very welcome on such a hot day. Like everyone else Periwinkle drank thirstily.

Once the food had been eaten and the water had been drunk the grape pickers went back to the field. All afternoon they continued to pick the grapes. Periwinkle had never worked so hard.

It was almost dark by the time the last of the grapes had been picked. The grape pickers took their leave, returning across the fields to their own farms and houses.

Periwinkle felt very weary and, as he was wondering where he might spend the night, along came Mr Charpentier on his shiny blue tractor so Periwinkle asked him very politely whether it would be possible for him to sleep underneath one of the grape trees.

"I will not need anything to eat", he assured him. "I ate well from the feast at lunchtime and I still have some of my sandwiches left which will make me some breakfast."

Mr Charpentier threw up his hands in horror. "No, no Periwinkle! That won't do at all! You've worked hard today and you're welcome to spend the night in my barn. You will be comfortable there in the hay and my wife will find you something to eat."

That sounded very satisfactory to Periwinkle who climbed up onto the tractor once more which took him to Mr Charpentier's barn where he did indeed find some comfortable hay. Mrs Charpentier brought him more bread and cheese and some of that lovely cool water that he had enjoyed at lunchtime.

Periwinkle enjoyed his supper and then settled cosily into his bed of hay where he was soon peacefully asleep.

Periwinkle makes wine

After a comfortable night in Mr Charpentier's barn, Periwinkle woke early the next morning. He stretched his arms wide and into the air as was his usual habit. Then he stopped and un-stretched them slowly and carefully as it occurred to him that they felt a bit strange.

He winced.

"Sore this morning are you?" came the voice of Mr Charpentier who appeared through the door of the barn with more bread and cheese, a cup of water and, to Periwinkle's delight, a little plate of acorns.

"It's hard work picking grapes. Makes you ache all over. Always feels worse the day after. And the sun has made you go very pink, if you don't mind me saying so."

Mr Charpentier sat down on the hay next to Periwinkle.

"I thought I'd have breakfast with you and we can talk a while. I've been thinking about your exploration. It sounds very exciting so tell me more about it."

Between mouthfuls of acorns and cheese, Periwinkle talked about some of his adventures. Mr Charpentier listened carefully. Eventually, when Periwinkle stopped for breath, Mr Charpentier looked at him thoughtfully.

"That sounds very exciting Periwinkle. But tell me: How will you know when you have reached somewhere that hasn't been found before? I mean, if you've found it then maybe other people have found it too. It's not going to have a sign on it saying 'land that hasn't been found yet'. Because if it's got a sign on it then it means someone else has already found it."

That was an interesting point and was something that Periwinkle hadn't considered before. He wondered how all the other famous explorers had known that they were the first ones ever to set foot somewhere.

"Hmm," he started. "Well I …" and his voice tailed off.

He chewed more bread and he nibbled another acorn. As always food cheered him up and, not being a piglet who worried too much about questions that he couldn't answer, he came to a conclusion.

"I don't know the answer to your question at the moment but I have a lot of exploring still to do in Europe and a long way to go before I even get to Egypt. I am sure that I will have worked out the answer by the time I get there."

He brightened further. "And besides, I am making lots of discoveries and learning lots of things. I like to learn about things. Speaking of which, please tell me what will happen with the grapes that we picked yesterday."

He listened as Mr Charpentier told him that the grapes would be tipped into big containers. The neighbours who had helped to pick the grapes yesterday would come back today. They would take off their shoes and socks and roll up their trousers or hold up their skirts. They would climb into the big containers and would jump up and down on the grapes until all the juices ran out. Some other things would then be added to the grape juice and in a few months' time it would turn into wine.

Periwinkle began to laugh. He laughed and laughed until tears came from his eyes and he thought his sides might split. It seemed to him that the farmer was having a jolly good joke.

"No, honestly Periwinkle. That's how we make wine from grapes."

Periwinkle stopped laughing. He stared at Mr Charpentier with his mouth wide open.

"Really?"

Mr Charpentier assured him that that was the case.

An idea began to form itself in Periwinkle's mind. He had planned to continue his journeying today but making wine sounded like a lot of fun and it would be another marvellous adventure that he would be able to tell people about.

"Might I have a go do you think?"

"You can if you'd like to. If you're not too sore from all the grape-picking yesterday."

Periwinkle found that some breakfast and the promise of another fine adventure had miraculously made his aches seem not as bad as when he had first woken up.

"I would very much like to," he confirmed.

Mr Charpentier laughed and clapped his hands.

"Come along then. Let's go make wine."

After packing the remaining acorns into his duffel bag for later Periwinkle went with the farmer to another barn where the people he had met the day before were waiting in their bare feet. The men had their trousers rolled up and the ladies had their skirts held high.

Huge baskets of grapes stood next to long troughs which were set out along the middle of the barn. Some of the men helped Mr Charpentier to empty the baskets into the troughs and, when they had been emptied, everybody began to climb on top of the grapes.

Periwinkle found the grapes were cool under his feet and they squashed easily as he moved around, jumping up and down like the others were doing.

The man who had played the guitar in the field the day before played some tunes and everybody danced around. The juice from the grapes splashed up their legs but nobody seemed to mind. If yesterday had felt like a party then today was even more of a party thought Periwinkle as he danced with everyone else.

One of the men took off the flat hat that he was wearing and put it onto Periwinkle's head. "A present for my young pigling friend." Everyone applauded and told Periwinkle that he looked "magnifique" which Periwinkle knew was a good thing.

He had an absolutely splendid time and was almost sad when the last of the grapes had been squashed.

"Will this really turn into wine?" he asked as Mr Charpentier helped him out of the trough.

"It certainly will Periwinkle. And this year I'll be able to say that my wine was made by a piglet. I might even name it after you! How about that?"

Periwinkle liked the idea of that even if he still wasn't totally convinced that this wasn't all some huge joke and had nothing to do with making wine.

He liked even more that, whilst they had been jumping on the grapes, another table had been set with food.

As before, there were stone jugs on the table. Periwinkle reached for one, eager to have some of that lovely cool water. He poured some of it into a glass. Something about it didn't seem quite right but Periwinkle was thirsty so he tipped the contents of the glass straight into his mouth. It hit the back of his throat and made him cough.

"What on earth …" he spluttered. "What's wrong with that water?"

The people nearby laughed.

"That's wine, young pigling. It's what we made last year. Have more!" and they poured him another glass.

Periwinkle wasn't entirely sure that piglets were meant to drink wine and, besides, he'd seen what it had done to Mr Labouche, the farmer who forgot to look after his goats after he'd been drinking wine. So he left his glass untouched and, after a while, he left the table and went in search of water as he was still thirsty.

He looked back to the table where everyone was eating and talking and drinking and slapping each other on the back and laughing. It looked as though the noisy party would go on for many hours

Periwinkle decided it was time that he got back on his travels. He had enjoyed two very exciting days and he had new adventures to talk about. But he hadn't made much progress on his journey.

Nobody saw him leave and he was sure they wouldn't miss him as they were all having such a jolly good time. He slipped away from the farmhouse and the fields of grape trees. He put his new hat into his duffel bag, checked his little compass and set off once again in a sort of south and east direction towards Egypt.

PERIWINKLE PIG AND THE TRAIN

Periwinkle finds it difficult to see

Periwinkle had left his home in England with the aim of exploring the world. He was heading first to Egypt, and was hoping to go even further than that and perhaps discover places that had never been discovered before.

So far on his travels he had been blessed with good weather. Periwinkle was pleased that it hadn't rained too often. He didn't much like rain. It makes you wet and getting wet is fun when you're having a bath or rolling around in a puddle with your friends. It isn't nearly as much fun when you're exploring and on your way to have adventures. Occasionally it had rained overnight and had been just enough to wash away the dust and make the fields and the flowers gleam brightly again so that everything looked colourful once more.

Waking one morning after another good night's sleep, Periwinkle slowly opened his eyes and saw to his surprise that the world had turned grey. Or, to be exact, the world immediately around him had turned grey and felt a bit damp. Any further than that had simply disappeared!

"How can the world just disappear like that?" he wondered sleepily to himself. "It was there when I went to sleep. And someone has rubbed out all the colours too. Perhaps I am still asleep and this is just a dream."

He shook his head a few times. No, he was definitely awake and it all looked exactly as it had done when he had first opened his eyes – grey and disappeared. But shaking his head had woken him up a bit more and he now realised that he was in fact surrounded by fog. Very thick fog.

It was going to be a difficult day for exploring, he realised.

He reached into his duffel bag and pulled out his clever little compass, the one that always pointed to north, no matter how many times you turned it around. He wasn't sure whether his compass would work inside all this fog but it did and so he set off in the direction that it told him was sort of south and east.

As he walked the fog walked with him and seemed to wrap itself around him. It felt to Periwinkle that it was even creeping inside his clothing.

He tried putting on the hat that he'd been given when he was making wine. He hoped it might keep his head dry but he found that a piglet's ears aren't really made for wearing that sort of hat so he took it off and put it back into his duffel bag.

He really couldn't see very far in front of him at all … or to the side … or behind him when he took a brief look over his shoulder. He had to stop more often than usual to check his compass to make sure that he was still heading sort of south and east. And when he got out his compass he also took out a sandwich or a biscuit and he had to nibble it very quickly before the fog could make it damp which is what fog does to sandwiches and biscuits.

Usually as he walked along country lanes Periwinkle enjoyed listening to the noises of the countryside. He liked to hear the birds twittering in the hedges and the sheep baaing and the cows mooing in the fields and the sort of jumpy little noise that rabbits made as they hopped along nearby. Today there was no noise. It was as though the fog had filled up his ears like cotton wool and had made him unable to hear anything.

Sometimes Periwinkle could see a bright circle in the sky which he knew would be the sun but it was high above all the fog and it was doing a particularly bad job at brightening things up.

"It is certainly a very grey day," Periwinkle told a signpost as he passed it.

It felt like the sort of day when there might be witches around. Not that Periwinkle had ever met a witch. He didn't believe that witches really existed but he had read stories about them and in those stories it always seemed to be foggy. Like today.

He laughed to himself, feeling embarrassed at thinking such thoughts.

"How silly I am to be thinking about witches!" he told himself very sternly.

"Where's a witch?" came a grumpy-sounding voice from further along the lane.

Periwinkle jumped in surprise. He peered through the fog and could vaguely make out the outline of a tree. He couldn't see anyone else around and knew it wasn't the tree that was speaking. It must be someone, or something, in the tree he concluded.

"Oh hello there! Are you a bird?" he asked in just a little voice because he felt a bit silly talking to someone that he couldn't even see. It wasn't the same as talking to yourself because at least then you know who it is that you're talking to.

"Of course I'm a bird," came the grumpy answer. "I'm sitting in a tree. What else do you think I'd be? I'm a magpie and right now I'm not very happy. I have places to go to and things to do today and now I can't go anywhere because of this blooming fog. Can't see a thing through it."

Periwinkle was a bit surprised. "But I thought birds had a good sense of direction?" he asked.

"Yes of course we have a good sense of direction. I, in particular, have an excellent sense of direction. I never get lost. Never," added the bird emphatically. "But I can't fly if I can't see where I'm going. I could fly into anything … trees, buildings, mountains … and then I'd hurt myself."

Periwinkle thought it was unlikely that the bird would fly into a mountain. He was almost certain that there weren't any mountains nearby. But he wasn't going to get into an argument with someone that he couldn't even see.

"I am an explorer and I'm not going to let a bit of fog stop my exploring," he announced.

"Not a good day for exploring," replied the magpie.

"Perhaps not but I am on my way to Egypt so all I have to do is head sort of south and east."

"That's easy to say" persisted the magpie. "But how can you tell which way that is when it's so foggy? I bet you don't know do you?"

"I know exactly which way is south and east," stated Periwinkle very confidently. "In fact," he added as a thought occurred to him. "I have a long piece of string in my duffel bag and if you would like to hold onto one end of that I will take the other end and pull you along with me until the fog clears and you can see where you are."

"A piece of string?" shrieked the magpie. "You want me to hold onto a piece of string? I'm not a dog you know. No, I'll just stay here and wait for the fog to go away. I won't fly into anything if I'm sitting in a tree."

Periwinkle realised he was wasting his time. Some people just don't want to be helped.

"I still cannot see you my little feathered friend but it is time that I said goodbye. You stay in your tree until the fog clears if you wish but I am going to continue my journeying."

The magpie muttered something in reply. Periwinkle didn't think it sounded like "farewell" or "good luck" but, as he couldn't even see the bird, he just called a final goodbye and set off along the road. He was happy to continue exploring with the help of his clever little compass which never let him down, even in the fog.

Periwinkle has a sleepless night

Periwinkle usually slept well. Most nights he fell asleep almost as soon as he lay down and he knew nothing else until he woke up in daylight ready to start a new day of adventuring. But one night was different. He couldn't sleep at all. He'd tossed and he'd turned. He'd tried to think of nothing at all but it's very hard to think of nothing at all because when you're thinking of nothing at all that's what you're doing … thinking. He wasn't sure why he felt so restless.

As the sun woke up and began its climb into the sky Periwinkle abandoned thoughts of getting any sleep and decided that he would get up and make a start on his journeying.

He yawned and he stretched and he wiggled his ears a little to see if that made his thoughts a bit clearer (it didn't). He washed in a nearby stream. He nibbled a biscuit and as he nibbled he thought and he thought.

Suddenly he knew what it was all about.

When he had been in England Periwinkle had really really wanted to catch a boat to France. Now he was in France and had found it to be an absolutely fascinating place but it felt as though he had been there a long time. He did so very much want to find places that nobody else had discovered and he was unlikely to do that in France. It was time to head on towards Egypt which was still hundreds and hundreds of miles away. In fact, it was so many hundreds that it was probably even thousands and thousands.

He came to a decision.

"Today I will visit a new country," he declared very positively and loudly.

"What's that?" mumbled a hedgehog who, until then, had been sleeping peacefully under the hedge close to where Periwinkle had slept.

"Oh I'm sorry Hugo," greeted Periwinkle. He had forgotten that, as he was settling for the night, he had met up with a hedgehog who was doing the same. The hedgehog had introduced himself as Hugo and they had enjoyed a pleasant evening talking about this and that. Periwinkle always enjoyed the company of hedgehogs who he found to be surprisingly interesting little creatures. French hedgehogs, he was pleased to find, were every bit as interesting as English ones.

"Yes, I'm sorry about waking you, but I have woken early and there is a lot of day that I can use. Today I am going to leave France and visit a new country. Well, after I've finished my breakfast," he added, for explorers shouldn't try to explore new countries without having breakfast.

"How are you going to do that Periwinkle?" asked the now awake hedgehog.

That was a very good question. Periwinkle knew that France was a very big country. He had already been walking for days and days and it might be more days and days before he could walk out of it. He thought a bit and nibbled another biscuit to help him think.

Eventually he had his answer.

"I think, my little friend, that I shall have to catch a train."

The hedgehog wasn't sure about this solution.

"A train? A piglet catch a train? I don't think piglets catch trains."

"I don't think piglets usually travel on boats either but I did," pointed out Periwinkle. Hugo couldn't disagree with that because Periwinkle had told him all about it when they were chatting the night before.

"If you're sure about it Periwinkle. It sounds rather exciting. Another adventure for an explorer to have. But where are you going to find a train? They don't come down these country lanes you know."

Periwinkle was aware of that.

"I will have to find a station," he stated, sounding a lot more confident than he actually felt. "And one thing I know is that I won't find a station if I stay here all day so I shall wish you well and be on my way."

Fully awake by now, the hedgehog decided to walk with him for a while. He thought that he knew the way to the main road.

"Not that I ever go there. Not a suitable place for a hedgehog," and he broke off, clearly lost in thought. After a few moments he continued. "The point is, that if you get to the main road you will surely be able to find your way to a station."

That sounded like a good idea to Periwinkle, particularly as he didn't have a better one, so they set off, the two of them.

After not too long Periwinkle realised that the peace and quiet of the countryside was no longer as peaceful and quiet. He could hear the faint hum of cars which, he realised, must surely mean that he was getting nearer to a main road. As the noise got louder Periwinkle began to feel excited.

Not so the hedgehog who suddenly stopped in his tracks.

"I think I'll leave you to it now Periwinkle." He spoke in a shaky voice. "That's the main road you can hear." He shuddered. "I think I'll just turn back. I'm sure you can find your way from here, what with you being an explorer and all that. Good luck with your travels. Send me a postcard when you get to Egypt.

"And just one thing," he finished. "Be careful of all that traffic."

And so saying he turned around and headed back down the lane as quickly as a hedgehog's little legs would allow him.

Periwinkle watched him go, slightly surprised at this sudden turn of events, but then he shrugged his shoulders, pointed his nose back in the direction of the noise and started to walk again.

It was only a few minutes before the country lane came to an end. Periwinkle wondered whether to turn left or right onto the main road. His little compass was very clever at pointing him north or south or east or west but it wouldn't be much help in finding a station unless Periwinkle knew whether that station was to the north or the south or whatever … which he didn't. He was therefore very delighted when he spotted a battered old signpost which helpfully said 'Station' with an arrow pointing to the right.

"Oh thank you Mr Signpost!" he exclaimed with joy. He always thought it was polite to say thank you for any help that he got, even if it was from a signpost which was really only just doing its job in pointing the way.

He turned right, trying to ignore the noise of the traffic. Not that there was too much traffic at all and he wondered why Hugo Hedgehog had seemed so scared of it. There certainly weren't as many cars as there had been in Paris but Hugo had probably never been to Paris so he wouldn't know that.

Periwinkle walked on with a spring in his step. He was on his way to a station to catch a train to another country where he could continue his exploration.

Periwinkle catches a train

Periwinkle was walking along a road which looked to stretch on an awfully long way without any sign of a station but, at last, there it was.

The front of the station was made of bricks that were dark red and looked almost shiny. At the top of the building were two pointed towers with flags on the top. There was a great open archway, above which was the biggest clock that Periwinkle had ever seen.

It was all very grand and, in Periwinkles opinion, it looked more like a church or a castle than a station.

Certainly it was nothing like the station in Sunnydale which was the nearest one to his home in England. The station there was just a platform with a seat on it and a man called Mr Stevens who walked up and down and sold tickets for the two trains a day that stopped there.

Periwinkle passed under the arch and into the station. People were walking in seemingly every direction. Some people were even running. A few people stopped to look curiously at this piglet with a duffel bag over his shoulder. Periwinkle smiled and nodded a polite "Bonjour" to them as he had learned to do.

A huge board on one wall listed lots and lots of trains going to lots and lots of places. Periwinkle wasn't sure what train he needed to catch or even where it would be going to. He looked at the list of destinations. A lot of them sounded French and he very much wanted to move on to a different country that day.

Eventually he saw there was a train that was going to Germany. He hadn't thought before about going to Germany but he was sure that it was to the right of France on the map. Even if that was more 'east' than 'sort of south and east' it was vaguely in the right direction. It was definitely a different country and Periwinkle was sure he would be able to do some exploring there and maybe have more adventures.

Underneath the board was a sign that read 'To the trains'. Periwinkle hurried in the direction that it was pointing and soon found himself at a barrier. An important-looking man was standing there. He was wearing black trousers and a black jacket with a belt very tightly fastened around a large tummy. He had on a peaked cap and underneath his nose sat a very bushy moustache.

Periwinkle walked up to him.

"Good afternoon sir. I am Periwinkle Pig, Explorer. Right now I have explored enough of France so I wish to catch a train to Germany to continue my explorations. How much will a ticket be please?"

The man looked down at him.

"I don't know about an explorer but you're a piglet and animals go free. No charge!"

This was welcome news for Periwinkle even when the man explained that he would have to travel with the other animals in the train carriage that was just behind the engine. He didn't mind where he was on the train. He just knew that he wanted to be on it and on his way to Germany.

"Platform two," said the man. "Walk along to the front of the train and you'll see where you need to go."

The barrier opened and Periwinkle walked through. He found platform number two and there was the train. It didn't look much like the trains that Periwinkle had seen in his books. They were usually grey and a bit grubby and looked very old. This one was blue and shiny and looked as if it had just been taken out of a box that morning. It looked very solid.

Very sort of … serious. It looked the sort of train that might go all the way to Germany without even thinking about it. Periwinkle walked … and he walked … and he walked. Goodness it was a very long train.

Eventually he could see the front of the train and, just before he reached it, he saw another man in a black uniform who was standing next to an open door. The man saw him and spoke.

"On your own are you young pigling? That's a bit different but OK, on you get."

Periwinkle happily stepped through the open door of the train. He found himself in the company of a number of large geese. He noticed that French geese looked very much like English geese. Some of them had brown feathers and some were white and they turned their strangely long necks so they could see who had joined them. They observed him for a few seconds and Periwinkle wondered whether they were going to be friendly. He knew that geese weren't always friendly and sometimes made hissing noises to show just how unfriendly they were.

"Piglet are you?" asked one. "That'll make a change. It's normally just us and a few chickens. Noisy little devils they are with all that clucking. You don't cluck do you?"

Periwinkle confirmed that he never clucked. It wasn't something that piglets did.

"That's good," continued the goose. "Sometimes we get a goat or two and they do a bit of bleating but that's not too bad. I don't think we've ever had a piglet but welcome anyway."

Periwinkle breathed a sigh of relief. He didn't know how long it was going to take for the train to get to Germany and it would seem like a very long time indeed if he was in the company of some unfriendly geese.

"Thank you Mrs Goose," he replied. "I am Periwinkle Pig. I am an explorer who is on his way to Egypt and to places beyond. I have travelled from England and have had lots of adventures …"

His explanation was cut short by the extremely loud noise of a whistle. It was such a loud noise that it made him jump with surprise.

"I'm not sure you're going to get as far as Egypt if you're scared by a little noise like that!" laughed one of the geese. Periwinkle explained that he wasn't actually scared. It was just he wasn't expecting the noise and it had made him jump.

"They always blow a whistle when the train's about to leave the station." The goose appeared to know what she was talking about for, sure enough, Periwinkle realised that the train was moving. He was on his way to Germany!

"Where is Egypt anyway?" asked a goose with feathers that looked so brightly white that it was almost as though she had been in a washing machine.

"And tell us about these adventures," invited another.

So Periwinkle sat down and told them about Egypt and about some of his adventures. They were all enthralled by his tales of being an explorer and they agreed that Egypt sounded like a very interesting place and that there were probably places near to it that hadn't yet been discovered.

As the train sped along Periwinkle's attention was occasionally distracted by a door at the front of the carriage.

"Where does that door lead to?" he asked. None of the geese knew the answer to that, just that they weren't allowed to go through the door. "You can't go through there," they all told him in their various ways. But Periwinkle was an explorer and in his opinion the door was another thing that he should explore so he went towards it and tried the handle.

The handle turned. The door was unlocked.

"I'll just have a quick look," he announced and, with that, he stepped through the door and found himself right at the very front of the train.

Periwinkle gets an unexpected opportunity

The first thing that Periwinkle saw when he went through the door to the front of the train was a man behind an enormous steering wheel.

The man turned as he heard the door open.

"Hello piglet! Come to help me drive the train have you?"

Periwinkle laughed. "Oh no sir. I'm an explorer, not a train driver. My name is Periwinkle Pig and I have travelled from England. I've had lots of adventures and have enjoyed exploring France but now it is time that I continued my journey towards Egypt and that is why I am on your train today."

"Egypt? This train isn't going all the way to Egypt you know. But I'm pleased to meet you anyway. Why don't you stand here with me and tell me more about your adventures? To tell the truth I'd enjoy a bit of company. It gets quite lonely being here on my own for all these miles."

Periwinkle was delighted to have such an invitation. He didn't suppose piglets often got the chance to stand at the front of a train next to the driver.

"Goodness," he gasped as moved forwards. "What a lot of buttons there are for you to press and what a lot of levers there are for you to pull. It looks very complicated. Not like driving a car. … well, I've never actually driven a car but I've been in plenty when other people have been driving them. That doesn't look complicated at all but this is different. You must be a terribly clever person to know what all these buttons and levers do."

The engine driver chuckled. "It's not complicated once you know what you're doing. Why, I think even a piglet could drive a train."

Periwinkle liked the sound of that. Now he came to think of it, if he hadn't become an explorer, he'd maybe have liked to have been a train driver.

He stood next to the driver and watched, absolutely fascinated, as the driver held onto the enormous wheel and he pushed buttons and he pulled levers. When they came to a station he pulled really really hard on a very long lever that had a large round red knob on the end. That made the train slow right down and, with a great sighing sort of noise, stop in exactly the right place on the platform. Periwinkle particularly liked it when they were ready to leave the station again and the driver pulled a cord above his head and the train made a great 'toot-tooting' noise.

Many of the stations had beautiful flowers in big pots and in baskets which were hanging from posts and in long troughs that were attached to railings. They made the stations look very bright and jolly and Periwinkle thought how lovely they looked in the sunshine.

In between pulling levers and pushing buttons and stopping at stations the train driver asked Periwinkle about his journeying and Periwinkle talked about some of his adventures.

After a while Periwinkle became aware of a sort of buzzing noise which didn't seem very far away. He looked to see where the noise was coming from and saw a large bumble bee just behind them. It didn't look as though it wanted to be there. In fact, it looked distinctly annoyed.

Periwinkle guessed that the bee had probably lived in the flowers at one of the stations they had called at and had flown in through the open window whilst they were stopped. Now it didn't know where it was. That was enough to make anybody annoyed unless they were an explorer and were happy to be finding new places and not being too sure where they were.

The bee flew around and around. The more it flew the more annoyed it looked and the louder it buzzed. It waved its wings very hard and occasionally it banged into the window of the train and Periwinkle was sure that would have hurt even though it bounced back off again. He wondered whether there was anything he could do to help the bee but he wasn't sure what that might be.

Suddenly there was a yell from the train driver. "Ouch! I've been stung by a bee!"

He began to sneeze and to sneeze and to sneeze.

"Here Periwinkle … achoo … I can't see a thing when I'm … achoo … sneezing like this. You'll … achoo … have to hold onto the wheel for me until I … achoo … stop." He moved away from the steering wheel and dug deep into his pocket, bringing out a handkerchief that Periwinkle thought looked as big as a tablecloth. Not that Periwinkle thought about it for very long because it appeared that he, an exploring piglet, was going to have to drive the train!

He held onto the steering wheel and he pushed a couple of buttons to make it look as though he knew what he was doing. He pulled the cord that was above his head because he liked the 'toot-toot' noise that happened when he did that. He waved at the people who were at the side of the tracks but he only waved with one hand because he was using the other to grip the steering wheel very tightly.

The scenery flashed past and it seemed to Periwinkle that driving a train wasn't too difficult after all. He vaguely wondered whether he would be able to make the train stop in the right place when they got to the next station and, for that matter, how he'd know when they were getting near to the station, but he decided not to worry about that too much and just concentrate on driving the train.

Fortunately, before he really did have to worry about the next station, the engine driver finally stopped sneezing. He put his handkerchief away and stepped back to the wheel.

"Thank you Periwinkle. That was a close shave. It's a good job you were here or that could have been very nasty. You'd better stay here for the rest of the journey just in case Mr Bee had a friend with him."

So Periwinkle stayed at the front of the train with the engine driver for the rest of the journey. If truth be told he was a bit disappointed that there were no more bees and therefore there was no call for him to drive the train again.

Before too long the engine driver stopped the train at another station which was larger than the others that they had called at. He turned to Periwinkle.

"Righto Periwinkle. This is where you get off. We're in Germany!"

Periwinkle was surprised. It appeared that Germany was nowhere near as far away as he'd imagined it would be.

"I've got to take this train back to France," continued the engine driver, "And I don't suppose you want to come back with me do you?"

Periwinkle agreed that he didn't want to go back to France, even if there might have been the opportunity to drive the train again.

He thanked the engine driver for bringing him safely to Germany. They shook hands and Periwinkle stepped off the train. After waving goodbye to the engine driver and to the geese who were also getting off the train he walked along a very long platform and out of the station. He checked his compass to be certain that he knew which way was sort of south and east and he set off along the road.

As he walked he smiled. What an exciting day he'd had. He'd caught his very first train. He'd even driven the train. He'd made a lot of progress on his journey. Now he was in another new country where he could continue exploring and having adventures on his way to Egypt and lands beyond that were waiting to be discovered.

PERIWINKLE PIG AND THE FUNFAIR

Periwinkle becomes a mascot

Periwinkle Pig had left his home in England to become an explorer like the ones that he had read about in his books. He had spent time exploring France and was now in Germany.

On his travels he had found some comfortable places to stay overnight underneath hedges or trees. He particularly liked finding oak trees to sleep under. Acorns come from oak trees and sometimes, during the night, one or two would fall off the tree and land near to Periwinkle, making him a nice breakfast. Occasionally they fell onto him as he was sleeping and, if that maybe woke him up, he went quickly back to sleep with a smile on his face thinking of the lovely breakfast that he would have.

He woke up one morning under just such a tree and sure enough there were a few acorns nearby. He nibbled one or two and put the others into his duffel bag in case he needed them later. Suitably refreshed he set back off on his journeying.

As he walked, he thought. Then he walked a bit more and he thought a bit more. And if nobody knew what he was thinking then that was alright because thoughts are very private things. Unless you tell someone what they are – and then they become words rather than thoughts.

After a while Periwinkle's thoughts turned to why so many people were walking in the same direction that he was walking. And why they were wearing clothes that looked the same. Their jumpers looked the same. Their scarves looked the same. Many were wearing hats and those looked the same too. Everyone seemed to be happy and they were talking and laughing as they walked along.

"Hey, great costume!" called someone, pointing at Periwinkle and sticking his thumb up in the air. Periwinkle didn't know what he meant but, being a polite little piglet, he smiled and waved and put his thumb up too.

He found it all very intriguing and, even if he didn't understand what was going on, he found himself being caught up in all the happiness. He smiled and he laughed. He spun around and he danced a little. He made "thumbs up" signs to the left of him and to the right of him. And he thought to himself what a splendid afternoon he was having.

Just as he was getting used to the party that he was having, his new friends began to go through a gate. He tried to follow but the gate wouldn't move. He pushed and pushed and still it didn't move.

"You need your ticket," someone told him, showing him a piece of paper which Periwinkle saw was a ticket for a football match that afternoon.

"I expect your ticket's in that duffel bag is it?" asked a tall man with a kindly face. Periwinkle didn't mean to tell a lie but somehow he found himself nodding.

"I'll lift you over," offered the kindly-looking man and, before Periwinkle knew what was happening, his new friend had lifted him up and over the gate.

Some of his new friends went off to the left. Some went off to the right. In front of him a path went straight ahead. Periwinkle didn't know whether to go right or left and, sensing that his little compass wouldn't be very much help on this occasion, he decided to go straight ahead.

At the end of the path Periwinkle found himself at the side of a big field. The field had very short grass and lines painted onto it. Around the edge of the field were lots and lots and more lots of seats.

"Oh good heavens, I'm on the football pitch!" realised Periwinkle in some alarm. He turned around, thinking to leave, and saw a red-faced man running towards him who appeared to be in a bit of a flap.

"At last! The agency promised to send someone and I was thinking you'd got lost. At least you've got your costume on already. It's not quite the right costume but it'll have to do. We haven't got time for you to change. It's certainly very realistic."

He stopped suddenly and put his head on one side. He looked at Periwinkle a bit more closely.

"I say, you actually are a pig aren't you?"

"Indeed I am sir," confirmed Periwinkle. "I am Periwinkle Pig, Explorer and I am …". He got no further.

"Yes, yes, I'm sure you are and that's fascinating but right now I have a problem and I need your help."

He explained that he was the Manager of the local football team. Like all football teams, they had a mascot to bring them luck. Their team mascot was a pig which, in Periwinkle's opinion, was a fine mascot for a team to have.

"Well, to be honest, it's a man who dresses up as a pig," the Manager added. He continued to tell Periwinkle that the man who dressed up as a pig had got a cold and didn't want to spend the afternoon outside at the football match. The Manager had tried to organise a replacement but he hadn't showed up. "And now it's nearly time for the game to start. I tell you what – how about you be our mascot for the afternoon?" He laughed. "A real pig … now there's a thing."

Periwinkle learned that he would have to walk out onto the football pitch in front of all the footballers. During the game he would have to run up and down the side of the pitch and, if their team scored, he would have to dance around a bit.

None of this sounded too difficult to Periwinkle and, as we know, he was always keen to do a good turn for someone, so he happily agreed.

The team came out onto the pitch with Periwinkle leading the way. He ran up and down. He punched his arms into the air and did a little dance when his team scored and he put his hands over his eyes and pretended to cry when the other team scored. He enjoyed hearing the roar of the crowd. It sounded as though everyone was having a wonderful time, particularly when his team won the match!

The Manager of the team led Periwinkle to the middle of the pitch where all the footballers were having their photographs taken. He pushed Periwinkle in front of the camera and people took his photograph and wrote his name into their notebooks. Periwinkle gave them his mother's address and they wrote that into their notebooks too and promised to send her the photographs of him.

At last the men with the cameras left.

"You brought us good luck. Will you come for a drink with us to celebrate?" invited one of the players and the others joined in with their own invitations. Periwinkle thought about it but he was starting to feel a bit tired after such an exciting afternoon and he still needed to find somewhere to spend the night.

"Thank you but no. I am very pleased that you won the game but it is time that I got on my way for I still have a long journey ahead of me."

"Oh yes, I remember," said the Manager. "You're an explorer. Where are you trying to get to?"

Periwinkle explained about his mission to get to Egypt and places beyond that haven't even been discovered yet. "I'm not going to get there today of course but I would like to be just a bit further sort of south and east than I am at the moment and then I will rest for the night."

The Manager smiled. "Well Periwinkle, you've done me a good turn today so I'll do one for you. I don't live near Egypt but I do live a bit further sort of south and east from here. You can come with me, sleep overnight in my garden and then set off from there tomorrow."

That sounded very appealing to Periwinkle and the footballers nodded and told Periwinkle that sounded like a good plan and that he would be perfectly safe with the Manager. After a few more handshakes and slaps on the back Periwinkle and the Manager got into the Manager's car and set off away from the football ground.

Periwinkle had enjoyed being a mascot but was very happy to finish the day by making a bit more progress in a sort of south and east direction towards Egypt.

Periwinkle goes for a paddle

Periwinkle woke up as the morning sunshine began to warm his face. He felt refreshed and contented after a good night's sleep in the football manager's garden.

"I'm full of the joys of spring!" he cried as he stretched his arms wide. To tell the truth he wasn't entirely sure that it was spring but he knew that was what people said when they were feeling happy.

"I'm full of beans!" he added which definitely wasn't true. He hadn't eaten beans for a long time but, again, he knew it was something that people said when they were feeling in a happy mood and were ready to start their day in pursuit of adventures.

His words disturbed a couple of sparrows sleeping in the hedge next to him. They usually got up much earlier than this but they had been kept awake during the night by Periwinkle's snoring. They weren't happy to be woken up by him now.

"It's not spring," grumbled one of them.

"And what have beans got to do with anything anyway?" added the other in a sleepy, but cross sort of tone.

Periwinkle didn't think there was any need for them to be quite so bad-tempered.

"It's a new day," he pronounced cheerily. "A new day for new adventures."

He took a couple of acorns out of his duffel bag. He didn't have many left but it felt like the sort of day that would be even better after eating a few acorns. In Periwinkle's opinion most days were better if you started them with acorns.

He finished his breakfast, washed his face, checked his clever little compass to make sure he knew which way he needed to walk and he set off on his day's journeying.

"Goodbye my grumpy little feathered friends," he called to the sparrows as he left. That made them grumpy all over again as they had just managed to get back to sleep but, of course, Periwinkle wasn't to know that.

He walked all morning. He felt rather hot in the heat of the sun so he was pleased when he came to a forest where, he assumed, there would be some shelter underneath the trees.

The path through the forest was covered in pine needles which made it soft to walk on although occasionally one of the pine needles stuck itself into Periwinkle's foot, causing him to say a mild "ouch".

Once or twice Periwinkle saw the outline of a bird flitting through the tops of the trees and from time to time he came across a rabbit or a mouse but apart from that he was all alone and found it very peaceful.

After walking for a while he began to think that he could hear the noise of running water. Well, not running exactly. More sort of falling. But not falling like rain falls and not falling like out of a tap into a bath. It sounded like it was falling from a much greater height than that. It was certainly a very special sort of noise.

Periwinkle stopped to listen more carefully.

"That sounds interesting," he commented to himself. "I think I will try to find out what it is that is making such a noise. That's the sort of thing an explorer would want to know."

He wiggled his ears to make sure that he knew from which direction the noise was coming and off he set. The noise got louder. Periwinkle thought he could hear a splashing sort of noise too and, he was almost sure, voices and laughter.

He quickened his pace. Before too long he came to a gap in the trees and there, through the gap, he could see an emerald-green pool, surrounded by rocks and plants. Behind it a beautiful waterfall cascaded from the top of a very high rock. The sun was lighting up the pool as though someone was shining a torch over it and where the sunlight met the waterfall it lit it up with little rainbows.

Periwinkle thought it looked like a picture postcard. He was astounded to come across such a scene in the middle of the forest. In the pool there were people swimming and splashing. Some swam right up to the waterfall and went underneath it and got ever so wet. Everyone looked as though they were having an absolutely splendid time.

Periwinkle would have liked to join the people in the pool but, although his duffel bag contained lots of things that an exploring piglet might need – rubber bands, bits of string, his little compass and, of course, sandwiches and biscuits – he had never thought to pack a swimming costume.

He walked to the edge of the pool. It was so clear that he could see rocks underneath the surface. He bent down and dipped his fingers into the water. It felt cool and pleasant on such a hot day. He splashed some onto his face.

"Why don't you get into the water with them? You know you want to."

Periwinkle looked around and there, on a rock at the side of the pool, sat a large green frog.

Periwinkle agreed with the frog that he would very much like to get into the water if only he'd brought a swimming costume with him.

"Swimming costume? What do you mean swimming costume? You don't see me wearing a swimming costume do you? Here, watch," and, with that, the frog hopped into the water, swam around a little and then hopped back onto his rock.

"See. No need for a swimming costume."

"Oh no my hoppy little friend," replied Periwinkle. "It might be alright for a frog to swim around without anything on but it wouldn't be right for a piglet to do the same."

"Suit yourself," retorted the frog and hopped back into the water. For a moment Periwinkle almost wished that he was a frog. But then he didn't suppose many frogs were explorers and able to have adventures like the ones that he was having.

He sighed.

He sighed some more.

Eventually he could resist no longer. He carefully put down his duffel bag on a rock where he didn't think it would get wet. He rolled up the legs of his trousers and he stepped carefully into the water. It felt good. He jumped around a little bit and the water splashed up at him but he didn't mind. On such a hot day he would surely dry off very quickly.

When they saw that he was splashing around some of the people in the pool splashed water at him and he splashed water back at them. They laughed and he laughed and it was a lot of fun.

He noticed that the frog had hopped back onto his rock and was watching the activity in the pool.

"Not coming back into the water then?" Periwinkle called to him.

"No I'm not. And if you don't mind me saying so, I think it's time that you and your human friends here all hopped off home and left me to enjoy my pool in peace. I mean … I don't mind sharing it but enough's enough don't you think?"

Periwinkle hadn't really thought about it like that but, now that he did, he realised that he had been at the pool for quite some time and he really needed to make a bit more progress on his journeying.

He climbed carefully out of the water.

"Well my hoppy little friend," he addressed the frog. "I thank you for letting me have a paddle in your pool but now I must be on my way so I will bid you farewell."

He stamped his feet a little to shake off the water and then, with a wave to the frog, he set off again back into the forest to continue his travels.

Periwinkle looks for adventure

Periwinkle felt as though he'd been walking for ever. He knew from his maps and books that he would need to do a lot of walking to explore Europe as it is a very big place. Much bigger than England. So he wasn't unhappy to be walking. He knew it was taking him further on his mission to travel and discover new places, starting with Egypt but then perhaps even further if there was time.

No, he wasn't unhappy at all but, on the other hand, it was days and days since he'd discovered anything new or had an adventure. Maybe it was as long as a week. He knew that even the great explorers hadn't had adventures every day but he hoped he might have another one before too long.

In the meantime he just kept walking. He walked along lanes and through villages. He looked into fields and he went out of his way to look around corners that he hadn't planned to look around. No matter where he looked there seemed to be a shortage of adventures to be had. Still, he was walking in the right direction – sort of south and east – so he was at least making progress towards Egypt.

Around lunchtime he found himself next to a field that was filled with lush green grass. He could hear noise in the distance but it was quiet in the field. He thought it looked a suitable place for him to stop for lunch so he walked in through the open gate. The grass was very comfortable and the sun was very warm and, after nibbling a couple of biscuits, Periwinkle decided to close his eyes for a few moments in the way that sometimes it is very pleasant to close our eyes when we feel warm and comfortable and have had a good lunch.

He woke up sometime later and wiggled his ears and his nose. It seemed to him that there was a lot more noise than when he had gone into the field and he was fairly sure that he could smell something interesting … something rather like food.

He jumped up from his comfortable patch of grass and set off to explore where such noise and smells were coming from.

Just a little further along the lane from where he had entered the comfortable field there was a much larger field with a sign outside it saying "Funfair Festival".

"Here's a fine thing to explore Periwinkle," he told himself and, as there wasn't anyone selling tickets or anything like that, he just walked in through the gate.

There were lots of people in the field. Periwinkle walked around enjoying the colours and the noises and the smells and he loved seeing how much fun everyone was having.

There were stalls selling ice-cream and stalls selling biscuits and stalls selling things that Periwinkle didn't even recognise but which smelled very appetising.

There were people throwing balls into buckets and then being given large cuddly animals: Bears, parrots, dolphins and the like (but no pigs as far as Periwinkle could see). He wondered what the people were going to do with the cuddly animals. Some of them were even bigger than the little boys and girls that were trying to carry them.

Some people were playing musical instruments that made a sort of "oompah" noise and Periwinkle thought that the music sounded very jolly. The musical people were wearing shorts which looked to be made of leather and they had on white shirts and blouses with flower patterns on the sleeves and front. Their hats were green and from the top of each of them stuck a long white feather.

From one corner of the field Periwinkle could hear people shrieking but the shrieks sounded as though they were happy shrieks, not frightened ones, so he hurried over to find out what was happening.

The first thing he saw was people sitting in what appeared to be very large teacups that were spinning round and round. It made Periwinkle's head spin just to watch it.

Other people were driving around in strange little cars. Periwinkle didn't think they were very good drivers as they kept bumping into one another. It reminded him of the traffic he had seen in Paris.

A little further on he saw what looked to be space rockets attached to long metal arms. People were in the rockets which were going around in a circle and going faster and faster and higher and higher. Periwinkle thought that the rockets would surely take off! He thought that he would very much like to travel on a rocket one day but probably not one that was attached to a long metal arm.

As he stood watching the people on the ride, he had a strange feeling that he was being watched. He often had that feeling and he was usually right.

He looked round and saw two blue eyes looking up at him from underneath a cap of bright blonde hair and from a face that was full of freckles. Periwinkle noticed that the blue eyes looked very much as though they might burst into tears sometime soon.

"Hello little boy," he said to the owner of the blue eyes and the blonde hair and the freckles. "This is all fun isn't it? Are you enjoying yourself?" Periwinkle thought that was a friendly thing to say so he was a bit alarmed when the boy started to cry. He wasn't sure what to say next but was spared the problem of worrying about that for too long when the man whose hand the little boy was holding spoke up.

"Don't cry Oliver. If you don't want to go on it then you don't have to." He turned to Periwinkle. "He's scared you see. Not like his sister," and he pointed to a little girl with similarly blonde hair and freckles. Her blue eyes didn't look as though they were going to burst into tears at all. "Sophie wants to go on it. She's not scared of flying. I bet you're not scared of flying either are you young pigling?"

Periwinkle confirmed that he wasn't at all scared of flying. "You see," he explained. "I am Periwinkle Pig, Explorer, and I am travelling to Egypt and then to discover new places. I left England … well, quite a lot of time ago, and I am having all sorts of adventures."

"Can I go on the ride Dad? Can I? Can I?" The little girl sounded impatient.

"I tell you what Periwinkle Pig, Explorer," said the man. "You take Oliver's ticket and go on the ride with Sophie. We'll wait for you here."

As you might imagine, Periwinkle was delighted with this offer and, after thanking the man, he allowed himself to be pulled towards the start of the ride by a very excited Sophie.

They were helped into a rocket by a tall man without much hair but with a big smile. Sophie sat on the seat at the front of the rocket with Periwinkle behind her. It was a tight fit for Periwinkle as the seats were narrow and he guessed that they were made for human-sized people, not piglets, however small those piglets might be.

Once all the rockets had people in them, the man without much hair but with a big smile stepped away and pressed a button. Periwinkle smiled too as the ride started to move.

Periwinkle comes to the rescue

So here we have Periwinkle sitting in a rocket and, even if it was one that was attached to a long metal arm and wasn't going to go anywhere near to space, it was still something new for Periwinkle to do and a better adventure than he'd had for days.

The rockets went round and round and faster and faster and higher and higher.

Periwinkle looked down and saw that they were a long way above the ground. Though not, of course, as high as they would have been if it had been a real rocket.

Sophie gave a little scream from time to time but the screams soon turned to giggles. "Isn't this fun Periwinkle?" she laughed and Periwinkle agreed that he was having an absolutely splendid time too. He was sad when the ride started to slow down and he wondered whether they might be allowed to go around again but all too soon they were being helped back out of the rocket by the same man without much hair but with a big smile.

"That was quite an adventure wasn't it Sophie?" he commented as they walked back to where they had first met. "Your brother will be sorry he missed it."

"No he won't!" she stated firmly. "He's a real scaredy cat. He wouldn't want to have any adventures ever. Never never ever. Not ever," she added for emphasis just in case Periwinkle hadn't understood the point she was making. "Oliver could never be an explorer like you Periwinkle. I could be an explorer though. I think that's what I might do when I leave school. It sounds very exciting."

Before Periwinkle could answer, Sophie's father came up to them in a stage of some agitation.

"Have you seen Oliver? I left him here to wait for you whilst I went to get some ice creams and now he's not here. He's gone missing! Everyone's looking for him."

Sure enough Periwinkle could see that, all around, people were looking behind things and under things and to the side of things.

"Oh Periwinkle, I bet you can find Oliver," said Sophie, tugging at his arm. "You're an explorer. You must be able to find him. Please find him for us," she finished in a very small voice that sounded as though she was close to tears. Periwinkle realised that, although she had called him a scaredy cat she was actually very fond of him in the way that brothers and sisters usually are fond of each other.

Most people were searching around where the rides were and others had gone back to where the food stalls and cuddly toy games were but nobody had found Oliver.

Periwinkle thought hard and then a little idea began to form in his mind.

"I wonder," he muttered and hurried away from all the rides and the food stalls and the cuddly toy games. He went out of the gate and turned back towards the field where he'd sat down for a rest earlier. If he'd found the grass comfortable then so might a little boy.

He went into the field. Looked left. Looked right. He called Oliver's name but there was no answer. Periwinkle had been sure he would find him there so he sighed and even stamped his foot with disappointment. He didn't know how he was going to go back and tell Sophie that he hadn't found him. It was with a heavy heart that he began to trudge his way back to the funfair that now didn't seem so much fun after all.

He passed another field and, glancing in, spotted a little wooden building that was almost hiding in the corner of the field near to the gate. The gate was closed so Periwinkle felt it was unlikely that Oliver was in the wooden building but it wouldn't do any harm to check. He climbed over the gate and opened the door of the building. There, sitting on the floor with his back against the wall, was the little boy.

"What are you doing here?" asked Periwinkle very gently.

Oliver's words came out all in a rush. He thought that his father and sister were angry that he didn't want to go on the rides and he was scared that they might try to make him go on one and he really didn't want to so that's why he'd run away and was hiding.

"Your father and your sister don't care that you don't want to go on rides," reassured Periwinkle. "They're worried about you and they're missing you. Let's go back and let them see you're alright."

Oliver shook his head. "I don't think I can walk all that way again. I fell when I climbed over that gate and I think I've hurt my foot. Maybe I'll just stay here."

That would never do thought Periwinkle. There was only one thing for it. He turned around so that his back was towards Oliver.

"Climb on," he told him. "Hold on very tight and I'll take you back. And, by the way, it was a very brave thing to do to climb over a gate."

"Was it?" asked Oliver, looking just a little bit happier and Periwinkle reassured him that only brave people climb over gates.

Periwinkle set off with Oliver on his back. He carefully climbed over the gate and walked down the lane to the field with the funfair where people were still looking behind things and under things and around things.

Oliver's father saw Periwinkle coming into the field carrying Oliver and came running to meet them. Periwinkle gratefully allowed him to take the surprisingly heavy little boy off his back and into his own arms.

"Oh thank you little pigling!"

It seemed to Periwinkle that within minutes he was surrounded by people telling him what a very clever piglet he was to have found Oliver. Lots of them wanted to have their photographs taken with him so, of course, he gave them all his mother's address and they promised to send copies of the photographs to her.

Sophie threw her arms around Periwinkle and kissed his cheek. "You're my hero Periwinkle," she told him. "I will think of you and your exploring and hope that one day I might become an explorer too. Though not if I might get lost," she frowned.

Oliver let go of his father and also gave Periwinkle a hug. "I wish I was brave like you Periwinkle," he said.

"I expect you will be one day," replied Periwinkle.

Sophie's father shook Periwinkle's hand. "I can't thank you enough. Would you like to go on some more of the rides? I'll happily buy you some tickets."

Periwinkle shook his head. He had rather lost his appetite for the funfair now and, besides, it was time that he made more progress on his travels before finding somewhere to spend the night.

After a last kiss from Sophie and a last hug from Oliver and a last handshake from their father, Periwinkle turned towards the gate to leave the funfair. He reflected how strange it was that, at the start of the day, he'd been thinking about how he hadn't had an adventure for days. Now he'd ridden in a rocket (even if it was attached to a long metal arm) and he'd found a lost boy. It just goes to show, he thought, that it wasn't too difficult for an explorer to find adventures.

With that happy thought in his mind he walked on to continue his journeying towards Egypt and lands beyond that were just waiting to be explored.

PERIWINKLE PIG AND THE MOUNTAIN

Periwinkle hears the sound of music

Periwinkle Pig was pleased that he had decided to become an explorer. Since leaving his home in England he had travelled a long long way and had many adventures. He hadn't yet found any places that hadn't already been discovered but he was sure that he would before too long.

Occasionally on his travels he had talked to a friendly farmer or villager who had been astounded when he told them how far he had walked and how much further he still had to go. Many times they had offered him overnight shelter in a barn or shed and some had even provided him with food. He had found that, in general, people were very kind to an exploring piglet.

He set off one morning after a comfortable night in a farmer's barn.

For most of the day, he did nothing but walk and walk and walk. The road wound around a little so Periwinkle stopped from time to time to check his compass. If, when he opened his duffel bag to take out his compass, he found himself taking out a biscuit at the same time then who could blame him. He was doing a lot of walking and walking always makes a piglet hungry.

Sometime during the afternoon he reached a sign at the side of the road which made him catch his breath. 'Welcome to Switzerland'.

"Oh my!" Periwinkle exclaimed in surprise. "Switzerland! I've walked to a whole new country."

He smiled.

"A very small country," he added. He knew from his books and his maps that Switzerland was a lot smaller than England. He had found both France and Germany to be very large countries and he was looking forward to exploring somewhere a bit smaller.

He quickened his step. As he walked he looked around at the scenery, trying to take it all in. He thought that, even if he hadn't seen the signpost, he would have known just by the look of it that he had crossed into a different country.

For one thing all the roads seemed to be going upwards. Not steeply but enough for him to know that they were going upwards. They were harder to walk on than roads that went downwards but he knew that sometimes you had to go down and sometimes you had to go up. That's just the way it is with roads.

There was a breeze and some tall grasses at the side of the road were being blown around which made them wave as though at a friend who they'd just seen in the distance. Periwinkle waved back at them with a smile on his face.

He walked past fields with bright green grass that was studded with flowers including some pretty white ones that sparkled against the green background.

He passed a lake that was oh so blue. A bright blue that Periwinkle had seen in pictures of lakes in his books but he had never seen anything so blue in real life. It was certainly a very different colour to Brumbly Park Lake back at home in England.

Just behind the lake was a mountain. It was the sort of mountain that a child might draw if their teacher asked them to draw a mountain. It was all sort of pointy and the top of it was white. It looked so near that Periwinkle thought he could surely walk to it … though maybe not until tomorrow as he had already done a lot of walking today. Why, he had even walked to a whole new country which was enough to be tiring for anyone.

Sitting over the top of the green fields with the white flowers and the blue lake and the mountain with the white top was a pale blue sky with just the hint of a fluffy white cloud here and there.

From somewhere Periwinkle was sure he could hear music.

France had been very green and Germany had been pretty but this?

"It's beautiful!" Periwinkle didn't realise he had spoken aloud.

"Yes it is. Very beautiful," came a soft and musical voice. Periwinkle turned towards the voice and saw the big eyes of a brown and white floppy-eared cow looking at him across the top of a hedge.

"Oh hello Mrs Cow! I didn't realise I'd spoken aloud. I hope I didn't disturb you?"

The cow shook her brown and white head. As she did so Periwinkle could hear the music again. It wasn't music like a tune or anything but a deep tinkling sort of sound.

"Not at all," answered the cow. "I was just having a look around before settling down for the night. I like to look around. See what's going on outside my field."

She moved her head to one side and Periwinkle realised that the music he could hear was coming from a bell that the cow was wearing around her neck. The bell went 'clunkety clunk' and 'dunkety dunk' when she moved. Periwinkle was fascinated. He didn't think that cows in England wore bells that went 'clunkety clunk' or 'dunkety dunk'.

"Is this where you live then?" he asked. "In this beautiful field next to the beautiful lake and the beautiful mountain?" He felt perhaps he should find a different word to use instead of saying "beautiful" all the time but he couldn't think of one that was quite so appropriate.

The cow replied that she lived in the field with some of her friends. With a musical twist of her head she pointed her floppy brown and white ears towards a group of other brown and white cows that were standing a little further along the hedge.

"And tell me," invited the cow, "What is a young pigling doing walking past my field?"

Periwinkle introduced himself and explained that he was an explorer who was on his way to Egypt and to lands beyond that had yet to be discovered.

The other cows wandered along towards them and the air was filled with the noise of all their bells clunkety-clunking and dunkety-dunking as they walked. Although it was a very musical noise there was rather a lot of it and, if he was being entirely honest, Periwinkle felt it was making his ears hurt just a little.

"I would love to stay and tell you about the adventures I've had and look some more at your beautiful field," said Periwinkle. "But I have done a lot of walking. In fact this is the second country I've been walking in today! And now I really need to find myself somewhere to stay tonight."

Well, cows are kindly animals so, naturally, they invited him to stay overnight in their field and share their supper.

Periwinkle looked to where they were pointing and concluded that piglets didn't really eat the same sort of food that cows ate.

"That is very kind of you and I will be pleased to sleep in your beautiful field and perhaps have some of your water but I have my own supper in my duffel bag."

"That's a good thing!" piped up a cow that was standing a little further away than the rest. "Not sure we've got enough to share with a pigling. Greedy chaps piglings are!"

"Do be quiet Caroline!" snapped the cow that had first spoken to Periwinkle. "You're in such a bad mood today. This little pigling has come a long way and the least we can do is make him welcome. Particularly if he's got his own food," she added as an afterthought.

Periwinkle found a convenient piglet-sized hole in the hedge and crawled through it into the field. He drank some of the cows' water and he ate one of his sandwiches and then he and the cows sat down on the soft green grass and they talked for a while. Well, to be honest, Periwinkle talked a lot and the cows listened.

Eventually the sky turned dark. Not black exactly but a very very dark shade of blue. The moon and stars took up their positions in the sky and they bathed the beautiful field in a soft white light. The moon made the white top of the mountain shine very brightly.

It was all very lovely and Periwinkle would have liked to have spent longer looking at it all but he was tired. He said goodnight to these friendly cows, even though most of them had already gone to sleep before him. He shut his eyes and, feeling pleased with how the day had gone, he was soon fast asleep.

Periwinkle is startled by a bird

After a tiring day Periwinkle had slept well in the cows' field until he was woken by the clunkety-clunk and dunkety-dunk noises of the bells that the cows were wearing around their necks.

He was keen to be on his way to explore more of Switzerland. He rose hurriedly, nibbled a biscuit, drank a little water and then, after calling "goodbye" and "thank you" to the cows he crawled back through the piglet-sized hole in the hedge. Checking his compass to make sure that he was still heading sort of south and east, he set off once again.

The fields he passed were just as green as Periwinkle remembered from the day before and there were just as many flowers in them. Although it was a sunny morning the air was a little bit cold and Periwinkle noticed that the flowers had turned up towards the sun to get its warmth on their faces. He tried to do the same but, he reflected, it was one thing for a flower to do that when it didn't have to walk anywhere. It was very different, and much more difficult, for a piglet to do it without bumping into things or tripping over his own feet. Besides which, he might miss seeing something important if he spent the whole time with his face pointed upwards. He thought it was best if he concentrated on looking ahead of him as he continued on his way.

He passed more lakes that were just as blue as the one that he had seen yesterday. The sun was shining and as it shone on the water it made the surface sparkle like the diamonds in his mother's favourite ring.

Periwinkle was sure that he was getting closer to the mountain that he'd seen and then he realised that there wasn't just one mountain but two … no, three … no, even more than that.

"I shall definitely have to climb one of those mountains," he told himself. "Because that's what an explorer would do."

Before he reached the mountains he arrived at a pretty little village. Periwinkle was surprised to find that it looked quite different to the villages he had walked through in France and in Germany and, indeed, those that he had walked through in England when he first began his journeying.

For a start, all the buildings were made of wood. He was used to seeing barns and tool-sheds made of wood but not proper houses and shops. There was even a church that was made of wood and had a great big wooden clock-tower on its top.

What's more, the houses had flowers cascading from wooden boxes underneath their windows. Flowers in all sorts of colours; reds, yellows, purples, blues, pinks and lots and lots of white flowers like the ones he had seen in the green fields. They all looked bright and cheerful and Periwinkle reflected that some of the villages he had walked through on his travels would have looked very much nicer if they'd been filled with flowers like these.

Many of the shops were selling cake or chocolate and sometimes both. It made Periwinkle feel hungry just to look at the mouth-watering displays in the windows so he paused his wandering and sat on a bench to have a nibble of one of his biscuits.

Suitably refreshed, he continued his exploration of the village. All of a sudden a bird jumped out of a door on one of the wooden buildings and cried a very loud 'cuckoo'! It was just above Periwinkle's head and made him jump in surprise.

When he'd finished jumping he realised that he'd read about this in books. "It's a cuckoo clock. How interesting!" He didn't suppose that many explorers went out of their way to discover cuckoo clocks but he was pleased to have seen one. "I'm glad I came to Switzerland but now I really do need to get on with climbing up one of those mountains."

"You can't climb up it you know," came a voice at his side. Periwinkle looked around and saw a large dog standing a little distance away from him drinking from a stone trough. The dog was brown and white and, like the cows he had met yesterday, had big dark eyes and floppy ears.

The news he'd given came as an unexpected blow. Periwinkle had supposed that mountains could always be climbed.

"What do you mean?" he asked the dog.

"You can't climb up it. Too high. Too hard. You have to get a lift."

"A lift?" Periwinkle laughed. He'd never heard anything like it and thought that the dog was having a joke at his expense.

"Yes, a lift. Come on, I'll show you," and the dog set off along the street in the direction of the mountain. Periwinkle still wasn't convinced but, as he wanted to get to the mountain anyway, he walked along with the dog.

Before too long the dog announced that they had arrived.

"There it is young pigling. Now I'm going back to the village before another dog comes along and drinks all my water," and, so saying, he turned and walked slowly back in the direction from which they had come.

Periwinkle looked in front of him. Sure enough there was a sign that said 'Lift' but it wasn't like any lift that Periwinkle had seen before. It certainly wasn't like the one that he'd travelled in at the Eiffel Tower in Paris. It appeared to be just some chairs hanging from a rope. They did, however, seem to be travelling up the mountain and people were sitting on the chairs and the people who were getting onto them didn't seem to be at all concerned about this being a very strange sort of lift.

He walked towards the lift. A man in a uniform was helping people onto the chairs.

"No unaccompanied children!" said the lift-man as Periwinkle approached him.

"But I'm not a children … I mean, I'm not a child. I am Periwinkle Pig, Explorer. I have travelled from England and I would very much like to go up your mountain. We don't have mountains in England. Well, not very large ones," he finished.

The lift man looked at him more closely. "Hey, I say" he exclaimed in surprise. "You're a piglet! I've never had a piglet on my lift before. This is something for me to tell my friends. There you go Peritwinkle, hop onto this chair that's coming round now."

Periwinkle was going to tell him that his name was Periwinkle although he'd been going to be called Peregrine if it hadn't been for the man in the office being a little bit deaf, but then he realised that it didn't really matter very much and maybe he'd better just jump onto one of the chairs before the lift-man changed his mind. He stepped forward and, with a bit of help from the lift-man, he found himself sitting on a chair with a metal bar in front of him.

"Hold on!" shouted the lift-man as the chair moved away. Periwinkle thought that was probably good advice and so he held onto the bar and began his journey up the mountain.

Periwinkle goes skiing

Periwinkle had climbed up a very steep hill when he was in England but he'd never climbed a mountain. He'd never even imagined that you might climb a mountain by sitting on a chair hanging from a rope. Yet here he was, doing just that.

He found it a strange sensation. Almost like flying but not quite because there was a rope above him and not quite as high although high enough to skim over the tops of some very tall trees. In front of him he could see the mountain stretching upwards and upwards.

Totally forgetting the lift-man's advice to hold on, he opened his arms wide like a bird's wings and called an excited "Wheeeh!". But then the chair rocked a bit and he quickly grabbed the metal bar in front of him again.

As he continued his progress up the mountain he passed one or two birds and called a happy "hello" to them. He thought that maybe they should try going up the mountain on a lift that was really a chair. It would be far less tiring for them than all that wing-flapping they had to do.

Eventually the mountain stopped stretching upwards and Periwinkle realised he had nearly reached the top. He wondered how the chair would know when to stop but he needn't have worried because there was another lift-man in a uniform who grabbed hold of the chair and helped him to jump off it.

"Goodness," breathed Periwinkle. "I've travelled all the way up a mountain on a lift that is a chair ... or is it a chair that is a lift?" He pondered for a moment and then concluded that it didn't really matter because he was now at the top of the mountain and was having a very splendid adventure.

He was surprised to find that here at the top of the mountain there was snow on the ground and it appeared to be winter. In the village below him, which he'd only left a short time ago, it had definitely been summer.

Periwinkle knew that mountains had snow on them but he hadn't realised that there would be snow in summer. In fact, he wondered whether he had somehow time-travelled and landed in a different season which would be a very special sort of exploration.

He'd seen snow at home lots of times but this was a different sort of snow. It was much whiter and softer. Softer than a fluffy pillow. Maybe as soft as a cloud, thought Periwinkle, although obviously he'd never actually touched a cloud.

He walked around a little and his feet got a bit cold from walking in snow but he didn't mind that too much as he was enjoying exploring the top of this mountain.

When he looked out into the distance he could see other mountains with their white tops. And when he looked downwards he could vaguely make out the village that he had been in earlier. He recognised the clock tower of the church that he had passed and, as he listened, he was almost sure he could hear a faint 'cuckoo' sort of noise.

He could see paths winding their way down the mountain and there were people walking down those paths. He wasn't sure he would like to walk down the mountain. It looked to him as though it was an awfully long way to walk.

He could hear some voices raised in what sounded like excitement and when he went to see what that was all about he saw that people in brightly coloured outfits and woolly hats were skiing in the snow. He'd never seen anyone skiing before. There wasn't much opportunity for skiing in his village back in England.

"What a fun thing to discover!" he said to himself or, at least, he intended to say it to himself but he must have said it aloud in the way that we all sometimes do say things aloud when we were meaning to say them to ourselves.

"Have you ever been skiing young pigling?" asked a tall man standing close-by wearing a bright green outfit and a green hat with a ball of white fur on the top of it.

Periwinkle laughed.

"I have done many things, including walking on the wing of an aeroplane and even driving a train but no, I have never been skiing."

"Here, borrow my skis and have a try," offered a rosy-cheeked lady who was with the tall man and wearing a yellow outfit where the man's was green.

Periwinkle's first instinct was to say thank you but no. But then he remembered that he was an explorer and that explorers take opportunities to do new things.

"How hard can it be?" he reasoned. "You just stand on a couple of pieces of wood and off you go and it really does look like a lot of fun."

He thanked the man and lady for their kind offer and said he would like to give it a try. They put a pair of skis down on the ground in front of him and, once he was standing with one foot on each of them, the man pulled tight some fastenings which held his feet firmly onto the skis. The lady gave him a couple of poles to hold in his hands and explained that they would help him to balance and to change direction and Periwinkle knew what she meant because he had seen people doing that whilst he was watching.

When he was all set the man and lady helped to push him down the slope, telling him very reassuringly that it was only a gentle slope. "You'll be fine!" they called as he began to move with the skis slipping very easily across the surface of the snow.

Other people in colourful outfits stopped what they were doing and turned to watch this amazing skiing piglet.

"Bravo pigling!" they shouted and "Faster!" and there were even a few cheers and "woohoos".

Boosted by their encouragement Periwinkle felt very proud of himself. He didn't think there could be many piglets in the world that had ever been skiing. What a marvellous time he was having. He was even happy when he felt himself going a bit faster. And then a bit faster again.

It wasn't long though before Periwinkle realised that skiing isn't as easy as it looks. His legs wanted to go in different directions and the poles he'd been given weren't helping him to steer at all. In fact ... a thought suddenly popped into his head. But not just any old thought.

"How do I stop?" he shouted. It was a question that he really should have asked before he started down the slope. From behind he could hear something being shouted to him but the words were being blown away by the breeze as he sped on down the slope which, gentle as it might have been, now seemed somewhat steeper than he had expected.

Disaster lay ahead. Periwinkle saw what looked like a small bush not too far in the distance in front of him. He wasn't sure where it had come from but he was heading straight towards it. He knew without much doubt that he was going to hit it. He just hoped it wouldn't be too hard or spikey.

As he got to the bush he somehow managed to steer a little bit sideways and just clipped the edge of it but it was enough to halt his progress and to knock him off balance. He did a forward-roll, going upside down, then right again and then upside down, then right again. Over and over he tumbled. One of the skis came detached from his foot and landed further down the slope. He let go of the poles and they went somewhere else.

Eventually he landed, in a bit of a splodge, on his back in the snow.

He didn't move.

Gradually he began to realise that he was alright. He was still in one piece. He wiggled his toes and his fingers and they all appeared to be working. He shook his head and dislodged some snow that had settled on his nose.

He smiled. That had been fun. He'd become a skiing piglet, even if it hadn't lasted for long. He rolled over and over, making some piglet-shaped dents in the snow and he thought to himself what a fine adventure that had been.

Periwinkle discovers a monster

An encounter with a bush had brought an abrupt end to Periwinkle's skiing adventure and now he was lying on his back in the snow.

"Are you alright?" "You poor pigling!" "Are you hurt?"

Periwinkle opened his eyes. The people in the colourful outfits who had been cheering him on had seen him fall and come to his assistance. They patted his arm and a lady patted the top of his head and he wasn't sure what that was about but he didn't mind too much because he knew that they were only trying to be helpful.

He was pleased to notice that someone had retrieved the poles that he had let go of and the ski that had come off his foot. He wouldn't have liked to have lost those when they didn't belong to him. His mother had always told him how important it was to look after things that you have borrowed from other people.

Everyone was very concerned about him and he reassured them that he was unhurt.

"But I think perhaps I have done enough skiing for one day," he pronounced and they all agreed and helped him back up the slope to where the tall man and lady were waiting for him with worried expressions on their faces.

"What happened?" asked the man.

"We were so worried about you," added the lady.

Periwinkle smiled to show them that he was quite alright. "Thank you for giving me the chance to try skiing," he told them politely. "But I think perhaps it is more difficult than I had imagined it would be. I had fun though," he finished, giving them back their skis and poles. He shook their hands and they wished him well and then they skied off back down the slope.

Periwinkle decided to walk around a bit more before going back to the village. He didn't know how he was going to get back down the mountain but he didn't feel like trying to solve that problem just yet. Truth to tell, he was still a bit shaky after his tumble.

He ate a couple of biscuits to see whether they made him less shaky and he wandered along a path that had been cleared of snow. He wasn't sure he wanted to walk on snow any more.

Suddenly he stopped, wondering if he had really seen what he thought he had seen.

"Hold on Periwinkle," he puzzled. "That snow over there seems to be moving."

The snow moved some more and then, to Periwinkle's surprise, it made a fearsome noise. A roaring sort of noise like a wild animal might make. And then, as he watched, a large white shape rose up from the snow! He jumped back and wondered whether he should turn away and run. He'd read in his books about something called 'the abominable snowman' which was a sort of terrible monster that lived in mountains. Here he was at the top of a mountain and surely this was a monster he was seeing.

"I'm having lots of adventures today," he told himself but in a smaller voice than usual as he wasn't feeling very brave and he wondered what other famous explorers would do when they came face to face with a monster. He certainly didn't want to annoy it by talking loudly.

Suddenly the monster shook itself. Snow flew everywhere.

"What are you staring at?"

Periwinkle felt that was a strange thing for a monster to ask.

"Anyone would think you've never seen a sheep before," it continued.

Periwinkle hadn't realised that he'd been holding his breath but now he let it out in relief.

"A sheep?"

"Yes. I'm a sheep. A sheep that was asleep and now I'm awake and I'm wondering what a piglet is doing on my mountain. Piglets don't climb mountains. I can't speak for every single mountain in the world of course but I've never seen a piglet climb my mountain."

Periwinkle was so relieved that this was a sheep and not a monster that he didn't bother with the explanation about how he'd climbed the mountain on a chair.

"A sheep? I thought you were a monster!"

"A monster? Where?" cried the sheep. Periwinkle explained that he had thought that she herself was a monster. She looked at him with a very woolly stare.

"What a strange fellow you are. There's no such thing as monsters. Only in books and films … and sometimes in people's imaginations. But they don't really exist so don't you worry yourself about them."

Periwinkle was relieved to hear that. It's what he had assumed but for just a little while he hadn't been totally certain.

"But what were you doing under all that snow?" he asked.

The sheep, who introduced herself as Sheila, said that she had been having a sleep and when she woke up she found that it had snowed right on top of her. Periwinkle realised that the fearsome noise he had heard had been her snoring in her sleep! He remembered his uncle Peter snoring and, now he came to think about it, it had been a very similar noise.

With the mystery solved he relaxed a little.

"Weren't you cold?" he wondered.

"Cold?" repeated Sheila. "Cold? Have you seen the coat I'm wearing? Thick wool this is. You don't get cold when you wear thick wool. I'm lucky to have it. You want to get yourself a coat like this young piglet."

Now, piglets don't really feel the cold although, as they were talking about such things, Periwinkle realised that his nose was getting just a little bit chilly.

And, of course, he still had a problem to solve. He'd done some skiing and he'd met a monster that wasn't a monster and that was all very exciting but he'd had enough of exploring the mountain and he knew that he wouldn't be able to make more progress on his journeying until he returned to the village.

"Well, my woolly friend. I have enjoyed meeting you even though you scared me, but now I will say goodbye and leave you to your mountain."

"Please yourself," replied Sheila the sheep. "I still don't know why you were on my mountain anyway," and she turned away and walked off along the path with flakes of snow flying off her woolly coat as she walked.

Periwinkle walked back to the chair that was a lift and asked the lift-man there how to get back to the village.

"Most people get the lift up and then walk or ski back down," was the answer.

As we have already heard, Periwinkle didn't much like the idea of walking down the mountain and he explained that he had tried skiing but it hadn't worked out too well. "It was fun but I'm not sure that pigs were really meant to ski," he concluded.

The lift-man laughed. "I'm not sure that some humans were meant to ski either! But I see your point. I suppose there's nothing to stop you catching the lift back down again. Here's a chair coming round now. Hop on and hold on tightly."

Periwinkle hopped back onto the chair that was a lift and began his descent from the mountain.

Back in the village he was relieved to find that it was still summer and there was no sign of any snow. He'd had enough of snow.

He decided to walk on a little before looking for somewhere to spend the night. He opened his duffel bag to check his little compass and then set off in the direction that was sort of south and east.

Before too long he came to a sign that helpfully told him he was 'Leaving Switzerland'. It seemed to Periwinkle that he had only just arrived in Switzerland and now it was already time to leave it. But, he mused as he walked, even though it was a very small country it certainly hadn't been short of adventures for an exploring piglet.

6

PERIWINKLE PIG AND THE HIDDEN TREASURE

Periwinkle shines a light

Periwinkle Pig was pursuing his dream of becoming an explorer. He had never intended to spend quite so much time exploring Europe because, of course, it had already been discovered and he very much wanted to reach places that nobody had yet been to. Not that he was too worried because he was finding Europe very interesting and there had been many adventures for him to have along the way.

He was now in Italy and woke one morning with a feeling that there was something rather strange about his surroundings.

He opened one eye and then the other and tried to move them around without moving his head because another feeling told him it was important that he didn't move very much.

Suddenly a ray of sunlight burst through the canopy of the tree that he was under and lit up some droplets of water than looked as though they were hanging in the air. Only they weren't hanging in the air at all. During the night an enthusiastic, but possibly short-sighted, spider had created an impressive web between Periwinkle and the tree. The droplets of water, which often appear in the mornings before the sun has had time to chase them away, were lined up along the strings of the web.

It looked very beautiful but it left Periwinkle with a problem.

Webs are very important to spiders. They catch things in them which is jolly useful, particularly when those things are little insects that like to bite and sting. But that was the problem. Webs usually catch small things. It was almost unheard of, Periwinkle supposed, for them to catch something as large as a piglet. Even a little piglet.

If he jumped up the web would fall apart which would be a shame after all the work that had gone into making it.

"I'm trapped in a spider's web," he chuckled to himself. "That's an adventure all of its own and I haven't even got up yet!"

He reached out with one hand and, finding the bit of the web that was attached to him, he lifted it up and carefully attached it to a piece of wood that was on the ground nearby.

He sat up, only to discover that he was being stared at by a large spider.

Periwinkle knew that some people were scared of spiders but he didn't find them at all frightening.

"Good morning Mr Spider," he greeted the spider before wondering, a little late, whether it was in fact a Mrs Spider. It isn't easy to tell with spiders. Unless you're another spider of course.

"You thought you'd trapped me but I've escaped! I am an explorer and we don't let things like spiders' webs get in the way of our exploring. Nice web though," he added politely.

The spider didn't say anything. Periwinkle wondered whether he, or possibly she, was cross with him and maybe he was being glared at. That's another thing that's not easy to tell with spiders. He felt perhaps it was time that he left this place and made a start on his day's journeying. He hadn't had breakfast yet but he didn't feel like eating with the spider looking at him like that. He decided he would walk further down the lane and stop for his breakfast there.

"Goodbye my little eight-legged friend," he called as he quickly picked up his duffel bag and set off along the lane.

After putting some distance between himself and the spider Periwinkle did indeed stop for breakfast. Suitably refreshed and fully recovered from being trapped in the spider's web, he got ready for his day's adventures. He took his little compass out of his duffel bag, spun it around a few times and, reassured that it was still working properly, he set off to walk in a direction that was sort of south and east which was the way he knew he had to go to get to Egypt.

He walked all day along a very long lane that ran alongside a forest. He called a cheery "hello" to the creatures that peered out at him from underneath the hedges and to the birds that twittered down at him from the trees. Occasionally a car came along and he stepped to the side until it had gone past.

As he walked he was thinking about all the splendid adventures he had had since leaving his home and imagining all the adventures that he was sure were still to come. He was so lost in his thoughts that he didn't realise what time it was.

The sun which had been shining all day didn't realise what time it was either until the moon got up and caught it by surprise, at which point it got very flustered and took itself to bed all in a rush.

Without noticing it happening Periwinkle suddenly found that the sky had become dark apart from the moon which cast a silvery light along the lane. A little further ahead of him he could see a large white stripe on the road and two smaller white stripes. Strangely the stripes looked to be moving!

He quickened his pace and when he got nearer

to the stripes he discovered that they belonged to a mummy badger and her two cubs. The badgers were black but had white stripes down their backs and that's what Periwinkle had spotted in the moonlight.

Periwinkle had met a few badgers back at home in England and he had found them to be very interesting and intelligent. They read a lot of books and know about things that many animals don't know about. He hadn't met any of them on his travels because badgers sleep during the day and do their walking at night when Periwinkle himself was usually asleep. They also don't often walk down country lanes so Periwinkle was surprised to see them.

"Hello Mrs Badger," he said by way of greeting. "Why are you walking down the lane instead of through the fields and the forest? It can't be safe for you. I've seen a few cars and bicycles as I've walked along today and, if any come along now, they might not see you."

The badger sighed. She explained that she was taking her cubs to see their grandmother. She knew that it would be better to walk through the forest but the moonlight couldn't shine through the trees.

"It's so hard to find your way when there's no light. And these two," and she indicated her cubs who were clinging onto her hands, "They don't like the dark very much."

"Oh dear," sighed Periwinkle.

As he wondered how he might help the badgers, an idea planted itself at the front of his head. He unfastened his duffel bag and, reaching in, pulled out the object he remembered packing. He'd always known that a very bright torch would come in useful to an explorer. He hadn't had to use it so far and he was concerned about the safety of Mrs Badger and her cubs. He pushed the switch and the torch lit up. Everything was suddenly very bright.

"Here you are Mrs Badger," he said, offering the torch to her. "Please take this as a gift. It will help you to find your way through the forest without it being too dark for your cubs."

She protested that she couldn't possibly take his torch but Periwinkle assured her that he was very happy to let her have it so that she and her cubs could walk in the forest where they would be safe from cars and bicycles. She looked relieved and, with many thanks, the little badger family headed into the forest, lighting the way with their new torch.

Periwinkle watched them go and decided that it was time that he found somewhere to rest for the night. Without having to look too hard he found himself a spot underneath a hedge where the grass was soft and looked as though it would make a comfortable bed. He lay down and shut his eyes and, as he drifted off to sleep, he reflected on how pleased he was to have done another good turn for someone.

Periwinkle takes a day off

Periwinkle woke up underneath his hedge with a strange and not at all pleasant feeling in his nose and his throat. His head ached and he was reluctant to stir himself to continue his journeying.

He tried wiggling his ears which usually helped him to wake up. Today that just made his head hurt even more.

He tried wrinkling his nose but that felt most peculiar. It made it tickle a little, then tickle a bit more and then …. "Atishoo!" Out of nowhere came a very loud sneeze which clean blew off the fluffy heads from a couple of nearby dandelions.

The first sneeze was followed by a second. Then another and another.

Periwinkle had got a cold.

"Oh deary me," he moaned. "I don't feel very well at all."

Whenever he'd had a cold before his mother had tucked him up in bed and given him a drink of lemon and honey which soothed his throat. Now he was on his own, underneath a hedge and a long way away from his mother.

He sat up and thought about breakfast but discovered that he didn't feel hungry. He forced himself to have something to eat in the hope that it would make him feel a bit better. He always felt better once he'd had some breakfast. But not today. The biscuits made his throat hurt even more and the sandwiches seemed more than usually chewy.

"Being an explorer isn't much fun when you've got a cold," he realised. "I think I'll just stay here today and leave exploring until tomorrow. It's comfortable and I can sleep." He shut his eyes. "Atishoo!" he added.

At first Periwinkle found it difficult to sleep when he had to keep atishooing but he eventually fell into some sort of slumber.

He didn't know for how long he had slept but as the sun climbed high into the sky and blanketed Periwinkle with its warmth he gradually realised that he was awake – sort of. What's more he became aware of some hushed whispering going on quite close to him.

"Is he dead do you think?" asked a squeaky little voice.

"I don't know. Shall we just leave him?"

"No, we can't do that. Not if he's dead. We'd better find out."

"We'll have to prod him."

"Go on then. I'm not touching him. He might be dead!"

It all went quiet and Periwinkle was pleased because even a whispering noise was enough to hurt his poorly head. Just as he was drifting back off to sleep, two things happened: First he felt a sharp prod on his shoulder and, second, he let out another loud "Atishoo!"

"Eek!" squeaked a voice in alarm. "What happened there?"

"Maybe he burst when you poked him with that stick!" squeaked another.

Periwinkle opened his eyes and cautiously looked around him.

A couple of feet away two small brown mice sat on their bottoms rubbing their heads and looking dazed. Periwinkle's sneeze had knocked them off their feet and sent them flying.

"You're not dead then!" said one.

Periwinkle agreed that he wasn't dead. "I was asleep," he told them. "I am Periwinkle Pig, Explorer, but today I'm not doing any exploring." Well, that's what he tried to tell them but, with his sore throat, he didn't actually say it very loudly and one of the mice crept closer to hear what he was saying.

"You're a pig you say? You do look like a pig but you don't sound much like one. Pigs grunt and snuffle. You're sort of croaking. Like a frog. Are you sure you're not a frog?"

"He's a bit big for a frog don't you think?" added the second mouse. "And a bit pink. Frogs are usually green."

Periwinkle assured them that he was definitely not a frog, however much he might sound like one. "I've got a cold and my throat is sore and my head hurts and my eyes don't want to open properly and I ache all over and any moment now I'm going to … atishoo!" and he sneezed again so the two mice ran away a little distance in case they got knocked off their feet again.

"You've got a cold have you? What rotten luck. Is there anything we can do to help?"

Periwinkle answered sadly. "No, I don't suppose so. Not unless you can find me a warm drink and something to eat that doesn't make my throat hurt."

The mice looked at one another. They shrugged their shoulders. They scratched their heads in the way that people often do when they're thinking. They looked at each other again. Then suddenly they both appeared to have finished their thinking.

"Stay there Periwinkle and have another sleep," instructed one of them and then they both dashed off up the lane and out of sight. Periwinkle lay back down under the hedge and closed his eyes.

He was woken by a kindly voice.

"What have we here? What is a pigling doing asleep in my lane?"

Periwinkle tried to rouse himself to say hello to this kindly voice and explain that he wasn't feeling quite himself but, before he could do anything at all, he let out another huge sneeze.

"Oh, you've got a cold. You poor pigling."

Periwinkle opened his eyes and saw a lady who looked as kindly as she sounded. He tried to smile at her but another loud sneeze put paid to that idea.

"You come with me little pigling. My barn is warm and cosy and you can sleep there until you feel better."

Periwinkle liked the sound of a warm and cosy barn so, although it was a big effort for a piglet with a cold, he got up and followed her. When they got to the warm and cosy barn Periwinkle settled himself down in a pile of hay and drifted off to sleep.

It seemed like no time at all before he heard the kindly voice again.

"Here you are young pigling. Hot water with lemon and honey. Just what you need for a cold. And try the cake. I just baked it this morning."

He opened his eyes again and saw that next to him was a cup and a plate on which was a very large piece of cake.

Periwinkle sat up and drank some of the hot water with the lemon and honey. It made his throat feel a bit better and he tried the cake as it was a long time since he had eaten and he was sure that he must be hungry even if he didn't feel it.

After a while the two mice reappeared. They introduced themselves. "We're twins. But we're not identical twins of course," which surprised Periwinkle as he thought that they looked very much alike.

They explained that they had run into the kitchen where the kindly lady had been doing her baking and they had danced around in front of her. She had chased them out of the house and they had led her to Periwinkle.

"We often do that. While she's chasing me, my brother nips back into the kitchen and grabs a bit of food. Sometimes she puts cheese out for us. We like cheese."

Periwinkle thought that really these mice were just robbers. But on the other hand, he was grateful to them for helping him.

They all sat together and talked for a while. The mice talked about some of their adventures (which mostly involved annoying people and didn't seem to Periwinkle to be much like adventures at all). And, with his voice now not as croaky and his throat not as sore and his head not as painful, Periwinkle told them about his own adventures which they found very interesting.

Eventually the mice realised that the sun had gone to bed and it was time that they went home. With final goodbyes and, after wishing him good luck with his exploring, they scampered out of the barn, leaving Periwinkle on his own once more.

He lay back down in the warm and cosy barn. As he shut his eyes he reflected on how much he had enjoyed the company of the mice. He realised that he had been feeling sorry for himself in that way that we all do when we have a cold. We think too much about how poorly we are and it is better if we take our minds off it.

"I am pleased I had a rest today," he concluded. "I am sure that I will feel much better in the morning and I will start my journeying again."

And, so saying, Periwinkle fell straight off to sleep without even another atishoo.

Periwinkle meets a pig with a sensitive nose

After a good night's sleep in the warm and cosy barn Periwinkle was pleased to discover when he woke up that he was feeling a lot better. His throat was still a bit sore but he was no longer sneezing and his headache had gone. He was even more pleased to discover that the kindly lady had brought him another piece of cake and some water. That was just what he needed to prepare himself for a day of exploration.

After checking his little compass to make sure that he was heading sort of south and east he set off on his way.

The sun was shining, making everywhere look bright and shiny and happy and jolly.

Periwinkle walked all morning and found that he was getting very warm in the sunshine.

Around lunchtime he came to the edge of a forest and sat down gratefully under the shade of an oak tree to eat some of the acorns that had fallen from the tree and were on the ground nearby.

Suitably refreshed, he decided to walk on through the forest where it wouldn't be as hot. He also hoped that he might come across a few more acorns that he could pop into his duffel bag to make him a tasty supper that evening.

As he walked he became conscious of a snorting and snuffling noise not too far ahead.

"A wild animal!" he breathed. "I wonder what sort of wild animal it is? And whether it is dangerous?"

He knew that wolves and deer lived in forests but wolves and deer don't make snorting and snuffling noises, or at least Periwinkle didn't think that they did.

"I am an explorer," he told himself. "I am brave and I really should find out what animal this is and whether it might be friendly."

He walked towards the noise, taking great care to keep himself hidden behind trees and only moving forward after peering around them to check what was there.

The noise got louder and louder and eventually, peering round his latest tree, Periwinkle saw that it was coming from a very large pig. Except this didn't look like any pig that Periwinkle had met before. She was big and black with an enormous bottom and legs that looked like tree trunks. She had surprisingly small ears but the smallness of her ears was made up for by an extremely long nose. She was sniffing around the ground underneath a particularly large oak tree and occasionally she used her nose to move some earth out of the way and dig into the ground.

Periwinkle wondered what this was all about. He walked around the tree that he had been hiding behind and coughed to draw attention to himself.

The pig continued what she was doing. He coughed again, a little louder. The pig looked up.

"Yes? Did you want something?"

"I just wondered what a beautiful pig like yourself is doing rooting around underneath a tree in a forest when she could be in a nice field or a farm?"

"I, young pigling … I am a champion truffle-hunter. Come from a long line of champions I do. My mother was a champion. Her mother was a champion. Her grandmother was a champion. Right back a long way. But I … I am perhaps even better than they were."

She fixed Periwinkle with a stare and something about that stare and the tone of her voice made Periwinkle feel that he was supposed to be very impressed. And in fact, he might have been impressed if he'd known what a truffle-hunter was. Or, indeed, what a truffle was. The only truffles that he knew about were the ones that came in the boxes of chocolates that his mother and his Auntie Pink enjoyed at Christmas. He was almost totally certain that people didn't have to go hunting for those underneath a tree.

But, if he was supposed to be impressed then impressed he would be. "That's a very impressive record," he said which earned him a smile and a nod.

"I am very pleased to meet you," he continued. "My name is Periwinkle Pig."

"Good day to you Periwinkle. My name is Snuffles."

Periwinkle tried not to laugh. Snuffles didn't really sound like the name of a champion. Champions were called things like Champ or Rocky or … well, Periwinkle couldn't actually think of any other names but he definitely didn't think that a champion would be called Snuffles.

"Oh I can see you grinning," moaned the pig. "And what sort of a name for a pig is Periwinkle anyway if we're being critical about names?"

Periwinkle was going to explain the strange circumstances which had led to him being called Periwinkle but Snuffles was still speaking. "And more to the point, what are you doing in my forest? Not trying to steal my truffles are you?"

"Indeed I am not. I am an explorer and I am on my way from England to Egypt to discover …" He got no further.

"England? Not famous for its truffles is it?" interrupted the pig. "In fact I don't suppose you've ever seen a truffle have you?"

Periwinkle admitted that no, he hadn't ever seen a truffle.

"Watch and learn Periwinkle. Watch and learn," and with that the pig continued to root around underneath the tree.

After a few moments she stopped rooting around, sniffed the ground and dug down into the earth with her exceedingly long nose.

"What do you think of that?" she asked, pointing

to a small black object that she had flicked out of the ground. Periwinkle wasn't sure what he was supposed to say so he opted for honesty which is almost always the best thing to do in that sort of situation.

"What is it?" he asked.

"That, young Periwinkle, is a truffle. And a fine specimen it is too."

"But what actually is it?"

Snuffles explained that a truffle is related to a mushroom only it doesn't look much like the sort of mushroom that Periwinkle would have seen in England. She handed it to him so he could study it further. It smelt a bit strange but Periwinkle liked mushrooms so he bit into in and quickly wished that he hadn't. Firstly, because he didn't like the taste of it and, secondly, because Snuffles started to shout at him.

"Stop that! You're not supposed to eat it!"

Periwinkle wondered what was the point of a mushroom that you weren't supposed to eat.

"Humans pay lots and lots of money to buy these," explained the pig. "They serve them in fancy meals in expensive restaurants."

Periwinkle couldn't believe that a human would pay a lot of money for something that looked so unappetising and didn't taste much better but then, he reasoned, humans do eat some very strange things. Things that pigs wouldn't even think of eating.

"We pigs find them for the humans. It's our job. We've got sensitive noses and can smell things that are a long way away … or are hidden in the ground … like truffles."

Looking at the size of Snuffles' nose Periwinkle could easily believe that it would be able to smell things that were a long way away.

"And now I'd better get back to work young Periwinkle. There are more truffles around here that I need to dig up."

Periwinkle still wasn't sure he understood what all this was about. He preferred the sort of truffles that came in boxes of chocolates. But Snuffles obviously thought the ones she was finding were very important so he was happy to leave her to her hunting.

"And I, Snuffles, had better get on my way," he said. "I still have a long way to go on my journey. Thanks for the demonstration though. Very impressive. Good luck with your truffles."

He turned away and, with just a quick check of his compass to make sure that he was still heading sort of south and east, he continued his walk through the forest.

Periwinkle finds hidden treasure

After saying goodbye to Snuffles, the truffle-hunting pig, Periwinkle continued his journeying. He walked through the forest until he ran out of trees and then joined a quiet country lane.

Occasionally he had to step to the side of the road as a car came speeding along but for most of the time it was just him and the flowers and the animals of the countryside.

After a while he noticed that there were more cars and fewer trees and he soon found himself in a village. As he walked through the village he passed a policeman who was wearing trousers with creases so sharp that they looked as though they would cut you if you stood too close. He had on white gloves and his hat was flat with a white top. The buttons on his jacket were shiny and looked as though they had recently been polished. He had medals across his chest which Periwinkle thought must mean that he was a very brave policeman.

The policeman gave Periwinkle a salute as he walked past and Periwinkle saluted back although he wasn't entirely sure how to salute so he just did the best he could. The policeman smiled and nodded so Periwinkle didn't think he could have done it too badly.

It was only a small village and it didn't take Periwinkle long to walk through it and back out onto another country lane. A little further along he came across some woodland and, thinking back to his encounter with Snuffles earlier in the day, he decided to have a go at finding truffles – whatever they were.

He had learned from Snuffles that truffles were normally found underneath oak trees and Periwinkle liked oak trees because that's where acorns come from. He very quickly found an oak tree and there were a few acorns on the ground which he put into his duffel bag but he wasn't sure how to go about looking for truffles.

He remembered how Snuffles had pushed her nose into the earth but his nose wasn't long and pointed as hers had been. He tried to dig with his hands but the ground was very hard and he didn't get very far.

On the point of giving up the search, he spotted a patch of earth that looked a bit softer, almost as though it had been dug up very recently. He suddenly remembered something that he had packed before he left home. He opened his duffel bag and took out a large spoon with a bent handle. He'd always thought it might be useful for an exploring piglet to have a bent spoon with him. Now he'd found a use for it.

Using the spoon, he dug into the earth. After a while his spoon hit something hard. He dug a bit further and then, looking into the hole he had made, he saw a dark blue bag with a rope around it. The rope had apparently at some time been white but now looked distinctly grubby. He tugged at the bag and it came out of the ground.

He wasn't sure whether he should open the bag. It didn't belong to him and it was surely rude to open a bag that belonged to someone else.

He sat and looked at it for a few moments. Eventually curiosity got the better of him and he opened the bag.

He was astounded to find it was full of jewellery. A lot of jewellery. Gold bracelets and necklaces. Rings with jewels in them. Brooches that looked as though they had been made a very long time ago and were made of gold and studded with rubies.

"Oh golly gosh!" he cried aloud. "Hidden treasure!"

He then looked around to see whether anyone had heard him because he still wasn't entirely sure that he should be looking into this bag.

"But why would someone bury such fine jewels in the earth underneath an oak tree?" he asked himself. He didn't have an answer to that.

He wondered what he should do.

He pondered for a while and changed his mind a dozen times. Eventually he decided to go back to find the policeman in the village. He was sure that such a smart and brave policeman would know what to do.

He put the large spoon with the bent handle back into his duffel bag and, with only a small delay whilst he ate a biscuit that he came across whilst he had the duffel bag open, Periwinkle retraced his steps back to the village and approached the policeman.

"Excuse me sir," he began. The policeman looked down at him with a smile.

"What are you doing back here little pigling? I saw you pass a while ago and thought you were on your way to somewhere."

Periwinkle showed him the bag that contained the jewellery and explained that he had come across it whilst searching for truffles and that he knew he probably shouldn't have opened it and he was very sorry if the policeman was cross with him.

"But I was hoping you might be able to tell me what to do," he finished.

The policeman smiled and threw his hands into the air.

"Well done! These jewels belong to Mrs Rossi and they were stolen in a robbery just last week." The policeman explained that Mrs Rossi lived in a large house in the village and was offering a reward for whoever found her jewels.

"It looks like that's you, young pigling", he added. "Let's go return them to her."

Periwinkle walked with the policeman to a large house with a solid-looking door. The lady who answered the door looked very grand and rather stern. She was wearing beautiful clothes but, he noticed, no jewellery.

"Your jewels have been found," announced the policeman. Periwinkle stepped forward and held up the bag.

The grand lady's face lit up and she no longer looked quite so stern.

"My jewels!" she cried. "How did a pigling find my jewels?"

Periwinkle was about to explain about Snuffles the truffle-hunting pig and the forest and digging with his spoon but he'd only just started when the grand lady continued.

"It makes no matter. I'm just pleased to have them back. And now I will give you the reward that I offered." She handed Periwinkle some money notes. He didn't know how much it was because the money notes looked very different to the ones back at home in England but he put them into his duffel bag and thanked her.

He was about to leave when a thought occurred to him. It had been a long day and it was getting late.

"I wonder," he started. "I wonder whether I might be able to find a small space in your garden to spend the night. I have walked a lot today and I am tired. I won't be a nuisance and I will be on my way very early tomorrow morning."

"You found my jewels," beamed the grand lady. "And I am so grateful to you. I have a lot of garden so please feel free to sleep wherever you will be comfortable."

He walked into the garden and discovered that there was indeed a lot of it. He looked around and found a comfortable-looking spot. He was just settling down when the grand lady appeared again with a tray of food. He ate some cheese and some bread and tried one of the biscuits. He found that it was delicious. Very much like a delicious English biscuit … only Italian. Truth to tell, Periwinkle found most types of biscuit quite delicious. You couldn't go far wrong with a biscuit he thought, happily putting the rest of them into his duffel bag for another day.

"Well Periwinkle," he said to himself. "That's been an exciting day hasn't it? Another day fit for an exploring piglet. Hidden treasure eh? Such adventures I'm having," and with that he lay down in his comfortable spot and, as was his custom, soon fell into a very peaceful sleep.

7

PERIWINKLE PIG AND THE BEACH

Periwinkle helps a frightened bat

Periwinkle Pig had left school with the intention of becoming an explorer and he was already making rather a good job of it. From the South Coast of England he had sailed to France on a boat and had then travelled through many countries in Europe.

Along the way he had picked up company with all sorts of creatures of the countryside; rabbits, hedgehogs, a fox and even a badger. They had all been absolutely fascinated to meet Periwinkle Pig, Explorer, and to hear about the adventures he had had since leaving his home in England.

He had walked through some very pretty towns and villages, some that were rather less attractive and some that Periwinkle just hadn't liked at all.

Walking one day he came to another village of the pretty variety. There were large pots of flowers on the streets and hanging beneath the windows of the houses. It was very colourful and it looked as though the village might be a pleasant place to live. Not that Periwinkle would live there of course. He was just passing through on his journeying.

In the centre of the village was a large and beautiful church. It wasn't as large as the ones that Periwinkle had seen in Paris but it was much bigger than the one in his village back home where Reverend Mark was the vicar.

This church was built from a creamy sort of stone which appeared to have sparkly bits set within it so that it looked all shiny in the sunshine. On top of the church were statues of men and women and angels. There were also a few statues of horses but, as Periwinkle had found in Paris, there weren't any statues of pigs.

The huge wooden door of the church was open so Periwinkle went inside to see whether the church was as beautiful inside as it was on the outside.

It was. Very beautiful. Its windows looked like pictures. They were made from different colours of glass and the sun shining through the glass was making colourful patterns of light on the stone floor.

Periwinkle had done a lot of walking already that day so he decided to sit down and rest for a while in this quiet and peaceful church.

There was nobody else there, at least as far as Periwinkle could tell, so he was surprised to hear a quiet voice saying "Hello". He looked around. There definitely wasn't anyone else in the church.

He heard it again. "I say, hello, can you hear me?"

It seemed as though the voice was coming from somewhere above Periwinkle but, when he looked up, he couldn't see anything. He felt a bit uneasy. It was strange to be sitting in a church and hearing voices when there was nobody there.

"Hello. Why can't you hear me? Look up. I'm here."

By this time, Periwinkle was quite certain that he wasn't imagining the voice. He looked up again and this time he could just make out a black shape that was moving around a little.

"Er, hello?" he called hesitantly.

"Thank goodness! At last! I thought you'd never hear me."

"Who are you?" called Periwinkle.

"I'm Bernard, the church bat."

When Periwinkle's eyes became used to the darkness above him he could see that the black shape had two long wings and a tiny body between those wings. It was definitely a bat and he remembered reading in his books that many bats live in churches.

"I've just moved here," went on the bat. "The previous church bat retired so I applied for the job and here I am. It was a promotion for me don't you know."

"Congratulations," offered Periwinkle, thinking that was an appropriate thing to say.

"Yes, you'd think it was congratulations wouldn't you? My mother was proud of me," added the bat which made Periwinkle smile because his mother was proud of him too. Mothers are always proud of their children. Well, unless those children do something very naughty of course.

"The problem," continued the bat, "is that this church is much bigger than where I was before and the ceiling is so very high. I mean, have you seen how far up I am?"

Periwinkle confirmed that he had noticed how high the ceiling was but he still wasn't sure where this conversation was going.

"I don't like being this high up. I can manage ten feet or so but anything more than that and I'm just not happy!"

It took all of Periwinkle's effort not to laugh. Who'd ever heard of a bat that was scared of heights? But, as we know, Periwinkle was a kind little piglet and he realised that the bat was very serious and sounded most concerned.

"Well, Bernard Bat," he started. "I am Periwinkle Pig. I am an explorer and, on my travels, I have had lots of adventures which have involved being high up. I've been much higher than you are. It's not really so bad when you get used to it."

The bat said that that was all very well but he

wasn't an explorer and he wasn't having adventures and he really really didn't want to be up so high.

"Let me think if there's a way I can help you," said Periwinkle and he started thinking.

"Hmmm," he said.

Then, a few seconds later, "Hmmm," again.

"I say Periwinkle," called the bat. "Are you still thinking? I don't mean to criticise but I thought an explorer might think about things more quickly than this. What with you having all those adventures and so on."

That seemed a bit of a rude thing to say to someone who was trying to be helpful but Periwinkle knew that sometimes people say things they don't really mean when they are frightened, so he decided to forgive the bat and carry on thinking.

After a few more 'Hmmms' Periwinkle had an idea. At the very front of the church, underneath an enormous window made of coloured glass, there was a ledge. He wondered whether perhaps there was a way of getting the bat to fly down to the ledge which was much lower and the bat would no longer need to be scared.

"Right-o Bernard, I've got it," he started. "You shut your eyes and I'll talk to you and then you can fly towards me. You'll know where I am because you'll be able to hear me but you'll have your eyes shut so you won't be able to see how high up you are until you're no longer that high up at all."

Now it was the bat's turn to say "Hum," only his was more of a doubtful-sounding 'Hum', unlike Periwinkle's thinking-sounding 'Hmmm'.

"But what if I bump into something? I might crash down to the floor. That would hurt. Couldn't you just climb up here and carry me down?"

That didn't sound like a good idea to Periwinkle.

"I'm sorry that you're frightened Bernard and I do very much want to help but I can't see a way of climbing up to you so my suggestion is the only thing I can think of. Just shut your eyes, take a little jump and start flying towards me. I'll catch you if you do fall … which you won't."

He began to tell the bat about his adventures, although he didn't talk about the ones where he had been on the wing of an aeroplane or up a tower because that might remind the bat to be scared about being high up.

After a few moments he heard a squeak and then he saw the bat make a little jump and begin his flight to safety.

Periwinkle sings in the choir

Periwinkle talked and talked as Bernard the bat made his way towards him.

When the bat was close to the ledge that Periwinkle

had seen underneath the enormous window with the coloured glass it was time for part two of the rescue plan. Periwinkle stopped talking about his adventures and called very firmly.

"OK Bernard, open your eyes now so you can see where to land."

The bat was a bit reluctant to open his eyes so it took him a couple of attempts but eventually he landed safely on the ledge.

"That's better," he sighed. "Oh yes, not nearly so scary here." He looked upwards to the ceiling. "Was I really all that way up?"

Periwinkle told him that he had indeed been all that way up.

The bat shuddered.

"I say Periwinkle, I think I might shut my eyes again and have a sleep until I feel less shaky. Bats aren't supposed to be awake during the daytime you know."

Without waiting for Periwinkle to reply he folded his long wings around his tiny body and fell silent.

Periwinkle thought that the bat might have been a bit more grateful for his rescue but he shrugged. He wasn't going to let a little thing like that worry him. He found a comfortable seat at the front of the church and sat down to continue the rest that he'd been having before Bernard the bat had called to him. He wasn't intending to drop off to sleep but rescuing bats is tiring work so perhaps he might just shut his eyes for a moment or two.

The next thing he was aware of was the noise of people talking. He opened his eyes.

The seats next to him at the front of the church had filled with boys and girls who were all wearing black dresses.

Further back in the church were lots of smartly dressed people. Men in smart suits and brightly coloured ties. Ladies in colourful outfits and hats. Some people had flowers pinned to their clothes.

Between the boys and girls in the black dresses and the people in the smart outfits was a man who had his back towards Periwinkle. He appeared to be wearing some sort of dress himself but Periwinkle knew it was a man because the back of his hands and his neck looked very hairy. His dress was in beautiful shades of red and purple and had gold threads running through it. Periwinkle realised that this must be the vicar of the church. Reverend Mark in the church at home wore a dress but his was dark and plain so Periwinkle thought this must be a very important sort of vicar.

It all looked interesting and colourful but it was a bit of a problem for Periwinkle. He was sure that he wasn't supposed to be there and, more to the point, how was he going to get out of the church to continue his travels?

As he sat worrying about the predicament he was in, he was startled by a sudden blast of music and then the boys and girls in the black dresses stood up and began to sing.

Periwinkle liked to hear music and singing and it all sounded very lovely to him. He forgot that he was trying to get out of the church and, instead, he stood up with the boys and girls and began to sing with them. Well, as we know, pigs aren't particularly good at singing and one or two of the boys and girls gave strange glances towards Periwinkle but he smiled at them and they smiled back and they all kept on singing and Periwinkle felt very happy.

The important-looking vicar turned round to look at them as if he felt perhaps something wasn't quite right but, before he could do anything about it, the music changed and a beautiful lady in a long white dress started to walk towards him from the back of the church.

Periwinkle realised that, without meaning to be, he was at a wedding and this was the bride. He didn't see how he could make an escape without attracting far too much attention to himself so he sat back down with the boys and girls and tried to make himself look very small (which wasn't too difficult as he wasn't a very big piglet).

The important-looking vicar said some words … and then some more words … and then even more words. The boys and girls in the black dresses stood up again and started singing so Periwinkle stood and sang with them.

The beautiful lady in the long white dress held the hand of a handsome man in a white suit who

Periwinkle knew must be the man she was marrying. Occasionally they glanced over to where Periwinkle was and looked a bit puzzled but mostly they just looked at each other and smiled a lot. They said some words and Periwinkle noticed a tear rolling down the face of the beautiful lady in the long white dress but, as she was still smiling, he guessed it was a happy tear.

This all went on for what felt to Periwinkle like a long time. Eventually the important vicar announced that the beautiful lady in the long white dress and the handsome man in the white suit were now married. The people in the church clapped their hands. The boys and girls in the black dresses stood up and sang again and then everyone followed the newly-weds towards the back of the church and out of its huge door.

Periwinkle thought this was the opportunity for him to set back off on his journeying but, as he was leaving the church, he ran straight into the beautiful lady in the long white dress who was coming back in through the church door.

"I was just coming to find you!" she smiled. She took his hand and led him to where the handsome man in the white suit was standing. He was surrounded by the people in the smart outfits.

"Here he is! We were right. There really was a piglet in the choir. Imagine that. A piglet singing at our wedding."

The handsome man in the white suit reached across to shake Periwinkle's hand and the other people patted Periwinkle on the back and said what a special wedding it was with a piglet in the choir.

"Will you join our wedding feast?" asked the beautiful lady in the long white dress and Periwinkle was tempted. The word 'feast' reminded him that it had been a long time since breakfast and he was starting to feel hungry. On the other hand, it was getting late in the day and he felt that he really should make more progress on his journey before settling down for the night.

"Thank you for the kind invitation," he replied. "But I must be on my way as I still have a long way to go and many adventures to have. I was pleased to sing at your wedding and I wish you a long and happy future together," which he thought was the sort of thing that should be said to people who have just got married. He waved as the beautiful lady in the long white dress and the handsome man in the white suit headed away to their feast.

As Periwinkle was getting ready to leave he noticed that Bernard the bat had woken up and had moved to a tree outside the church. The bat looked at him and began to speak.

"Thank you for your help Periwinkle. I'm sure I could have got down from that ceiling without your help." Periwinkle was sure that he couldn't. "But perhaps it's a good thing you were here. I say …" and he paused before going on. "You won't tell anyone about this will you? People might laugh. To tell the truth, I'm not sure this job is for me. I think

I'll see whether I can find another church bat vacancy somewhere that's a bit … well, a bit … lower."

Periwinkle agreed that a job in a smaller church with a lower ceiling was a sensible idea for a bat that was scared of heights. He wished Bernard good luck and set back off on his travels.

Periwinkle runs out of land

Since arriving in France Periwinkle had travelled in a sort of south and east direction, stopping occasionally to consult his compass to make sure that he wasn't heading in some other direction that wouldn't take him towards Egypt at all.

He now realised that perhaps he should have travelled a bit more east before travelling quite so much south because here he was at the very end of Italy and the land appeared to have run out. In front of him there was nothing but sea. Well, nothing apart from a pretty red and white candy-striped lighthouse.

The lighthouse was more like a tower than a house and had a light at the top that flashed occasionally to warn ships not to sail too close. It was on a rock some distance from the shore, surrounded by water which was crashing into the rock and occasionally splashing up so high that it made the walls of the lighthouse very wet.

Periwinkle thought how exciting it would be to live in a lighthouse but he quickly put that thought to one side. More immediately he needed to use his thoughts for a different purpose. He knew where he was and where he was going. He just needed to work out how he might get from one to the other.

He was fairly sure that a boat was going to be the solution. All the great explorers had used boats on their travels. He himself had already used a boat to get from England to France so boats were nothing new to him.

He could see lots of boats. Some were going out to sea. Some were coming back. Periwinkle needed to find out whether there was a boat from here all the way to Egypt. And, if there was, whether a ticket to travel on such a boat would cost more than the six pennies he had brought from home which were still safely in his duffel bag.

With such difficult thoughts troubling him, an easier thought was that he would like something to eat. He opened up his duffel bag and rummaged deep within it to find an acorn which he was pretty sure he'd put away in there.

He found the acorn but, more excitingly, also came across the money notes he'd been given for finding the stolen jewels. He'd forgotten about that and, although he didn't know how much it was, he very much hoped it would be enough to buy him whatever ticket he might need.

With a burst of optimism, and refreshed by his acorn, he set off towards where he could see the boats coming and going. A check of his compass told him that that was sort of east and he was pleased he was still going in that direction. He'd run out of south for the moment.

He walked for a while, enjoying the sight of the blue sea and hearing the noise it made as it crashed into the land. The sun was shining and it was the sort of day that made Periwinkle feel like singing as he walked along.

"Oh what a lovely day it is!" he sang. It made him feel happy but startled a crab that was sitting on a rock. She wondered what the dreadful noise was that was disturbing her peace and scuttled off to find somewhere more peaceful to rest.

Eventually Periwinkle arrived at the place where the boats were. He walked along looking at the signs which said where the boats were going to. None of them said they were going to Egypt.

Some distance away from the other boats was one which had no sign in front of it to indicate where it might be going. It was smaller and not as shiny as the others but Periwinkle harboured a hope that maybe this one would be going to Egypt. He walked up to the man who was standing next it.

"Good afternoon sir," greeted Periwinkle with a smile. "What a magnificent boat you have!" That wasn't strictly true but Periwinkle didn't think it was really a lie because it would truly be a magnificent boat if it would take him to Egypt. "I wonder if perhaps you are sailing to Egypt and, if so, whether I might buy a ticket to come with you?"

The man took a drink from the bottle he was holding. "Why does a pigling want to go to Egypt?" he asked.

Periwinkle usually enjoyed talking about his journeying but he didn't want to get into a conversation. He just wanted to know whether this boat would take him to Egypt so he opted for a shortened version.

"I am Periwinkle Pig, Explorer. And right now I need to get to Egypt to continue my exploration," which was true enough.

The man with the bottle shook his head. "No, we're not going to Egypt."

Periwinkle's smile faded.

"Going to Greece though," continued the man. "Easy to get to Egypt from Greece."

That sounded more promising to Periwinkle. He very much wanted to get to Egypt so that he could start looking for lands that had yet to be discovered but he'd never been to Greece and he was happy to explore there for a day or so.

"You can come with us if you want. We're not going until tonight though. Once it gets dark."

Periwinkle hadn't thought about going overnight on a boat but perhaps he could sleep whilst they travelled and then he wouldn't be troubled with a funny tummy from all the bobbing about that boats are prone to do.

He took out a couple of the money notes from his duffel bag. "Will this be enough for a ticket?" he asked, holding the money notes out. The man with the bottle snatched them from him.

"That'll do," he said. "And you'll need to help us load our goods onto the boat."

"Certainly I will," promised Periwinkle. "What goods are you taking?" he added out of interest.

The man with the bottle frowned and two other men who had been standing nearby listening to the conversation took a step towards him.

"Never you mind what we're taking," grunted a short man in a heavy coat. "Just give us a hand to load up and don't ask any more questions."

"And don't ever tell anyone about this," added the other.

Periwinkle didn't think that sounded very friendly and he wondered whether it was wise for him to travel with these men. But then he reminded himself that he was a brave explorer and this boat would get him closer to Egypt so he put his doubts to one side and resolved not to ask any more questions.

For the next few hours they worked hard to load the boat with cases and bottles and with boxes filled with more bottles and with wooden barrels that Periwinkle helped to roll onto the boat.

At last everything was loaded and the men sat around playing cards and drinking from bottles that they took out of one of the boxes. They didn't want to talk to Periwinkle which was fine by him and he made himself comfortable on one of the cases that he had helped to load.

Once it was dark the men put their cards away. The short man in the heavy coat untied the rope that was holding the boat to the shore and the man that Periwinkle had first spoken to grabbed hold of a sort of steering wheel. With a jerky movement, the boat slipped away from the land and began its journey towards Greece.

Periwinkle is very brave

Periwinkle awoke as the morning sun began its climb into the sky. He wasn't sure what had caused him to wake so early but a nagging thought at the back of his mind told him it must be significant.

So did a nagging feeling in his tummy.

He opened his eyes and sat up. He immediately wished he hadn't. He appeared to be on some sort of raft surrounded by sea and with no land in sight.

As the reality of day chased away the fog of night it started to come back to him.

He had been on a boat on his way from Italy to

Greece. A storm had come along and the crew had been drinking and were unable to control the boat. Periwinkle had been sitting on a packing case and, with all the lurching and bobbing around, the lid of the case had become loose and had fallen off the boat, into the sea, with Periwinkle on top of it!

He had thought about his mother and then shut his eyes. The storm passed and he must have fallen asleep, lulled by the movement as the water rocked his makeshift raft.

He shuddered at the memory of the storm and how frightened he had been and the shudder was enough to make his little raft bob around and he almost fell into the water.

"I'd be careful if I were you," said a voice over his left shoulder.

Periwinkle turned his head, being careful not to move too much or too suddenly. Behind him, perched on the edge of his raft, was a large seagull.

"You're a piglet, aren't you?" asked the seagull. "A piglet on a raft," she continued without waiting for any reply.

"I am Periwinkle Pig, Explorer," replied Periwinkle. "I am on my way to Greece from where I will travel to Egypt and then to parts beyond. Or I was until the boat on which I was travelling got caught in a storm. Am I very far from land Mrs Seagull?"

"It's a pretty long way on a raft," answered the bird, "You should fly if you really want to get there."

Periwinkle explained that pigs can't actually fly.

"I know that pigs can't fly," snorted the seagull. "But it's a shame you can't because that's really the best way to get to land."

She thought for a few moments. Eventually she spoke again. "You could always hold up a sail, because the wind is in the right direction to blow you to shore."

Fortunately Periwinkle had clung onto his duffel bag and he took out of it all the spare handkerchiefs that his mother had insisted he brought with him. He knotted them together and, with his spare socks and a few other odds and ends that he'd picked up thinking they might be useful, he managed to create a sail of sorts which he held up in the air. Within moments his raft began to move across the gentle waves.

"Just follow me," called the seagull, flying off.

Periwinkle soon mastered the trick of steering by dipping his feet into the water and he followed the seagull heading, he hoped, towards land.

After some time he began to make out the tops of palm trees and then their trunks as he neared them. Soon after his raft gently grounded on the pale-yellow sand of a beach which seemed to go on for ever to the left and right. The seagull veered off back to sea with a call of "Goodbye Periwinkle" and a wave of her wings.

Periwinkle stepped onto the beach, realising again that piglets' feet aren't made for walking on sand. Still, he wasn't going to make much progress if he didn't get off this beach. He didn't even know whether this was actually Greece and that was the first thing he needed to find out.

He started to take apart his makeshift sail, folding the handkerchiefs and socks and putting everything back into his duffel bag.

Suddenly he heard a lot of noise and, looking up from his packing, saw people on the beach. A crowd of people were running along the beach waving sticks and spears and grunting things that Periwinkle couldn't understand even though pigs are normally very clever at understanding grunting.

This wasn't at all what Periwinkle had expected.

Most of the people were wearing skirts made of twigs and leaves. One was wearing a tall headdress of feathers and fur and shining stones and Periwinkle guessed he was probably the leader of whatever tribe this was. He looked strangely familiar but Periwinkle wasn't sure how that could be the case. As far as he knew he'd never met a tribal chief before.

Periwinkle had no idea what was going on but he knew that he had to find some way of getting past these people.

As he tried to work out how he might do that a man appeared from between the palm trees at the far end of the beach. He was wearing pale-green trousers and a pale-green shirt and looked more like an explorer than a tribesman.

Once again Periwinkle thought there was something familiar about the man but laughed to himself in the way that people laugh when something isn't really very funny. It must be his mind playing tricks, he concluded.

The pale-green man stepped forward towards the tribesmen who were still waving their sticks and spears and grunting. The man had his fists raised and, to Periwinkle's complete astonishment, it looked as though he was intending to fight the tribesmen.

"He's never going to be able to fight them on his own," he gasped. He took a deep breath and drew himself up to his full height (which wasn't really very high at all). He told himself that he was a brave explorer and then, before he could think more about it, he dashed forward shouting "I'm coming to help!"

He was surprised but, to be honest, very relieved when the tribesmen stopped waving their spears and turned to look at him. He was even more surprised when some of them started to smile and the pale-green man burst out laughing.

For the second time that morning, this wasn't what he had expected.

Suddenly a bossy-looking man carrying a notepad appeared. He seemed to be very agitated. "What do you think you're doing?" he cried in a cross voice. "Why is a piglet spoiling my film?"

The pale-green man came towards Periwinkle who now realised that the reason he and the tribal chief had looked so familiar was that they were famous actors. He'd seen them in films that he'd watched with his mother.

"You thought I was in danger did you?" asked the pale-green man. "No, we're just making a film. Bless you for trying to help me though, you brave little piglet. But tell me, what is a piglet doing on a beach in Greece?"

Relieved to hear that he had actually landed in Greece, Periwinkle explained that he was an explorer who had been travelling on a boat which got caught in a storm and he had fallen off the boat into the sea on the lid of a packing case.

The actors gasped with horror and said what an incredible adventure that had been so Periwinkle told them about some of his other adventures. By this time quite a crowd had gathered and the man with the notepad had stopped trying to be bossy.

Everyone agreed that Periwinkle's adventures would be an excellent subject for a film! He had his photo taken with the two famous actors and they promised that they would definitely send those photographs to Periwinkle's mother which he knew she would be very excited about.

As day turned to night, the film people shook Periwinkle's hand and took their leave of him until, at last, he was alone on the beach. He decided to sleep where he was and resume his travels the next morning.

As he lay down with a starlit sky above him he smiled to himself. He had survived a storm. He was now in Greece, another new country for him to explore. He had met two famous actors and they thought that his journeying would make an excellent film.

"The Adventures of Periwinkle Pig," he thought and, with that in mind, he settled into his bed in the sand and fell into a happy sleep.

PERIWINKLE PIG AND THE MYSTERY OF THE PYRAMIDS

Periwinkle has a very close shave

Periwinkle Pig had left his home in England to pursue his childhood dream of becoming an explorer. He had walked a lot … and then even more than that. He'd been given some lifts in cars and vans. He'd driven a train. He'd been on two boats.

His plan had always been to get to Egypt and then to look for other places that nobody had yet discovered. He had a secret hope that one of those places might even become named after him!

That was all in the future. Right here and now Periwinkle was in Greece. He had been assured that it would be very easy to get from there to Egypt but he was going to explore Greece for a few days before moving on.

He wasn't sure whether he should still travel sort of south and east. To the south was water and, as his last experience on a boat hadn't worked out too well, Periwinkle hoped there might be a way of getting to Egypt that didn't involve water. So, setting himself in more of an easterly direction, he walked along the country lanes which, as they did everywhere, wound around and took him past fields and through villages.

One evening, after a long day of walking, he came to a village where some men were sitting and talking outside a café. The men looked up as Periwinkle approached.

"Hello little pigling," called one of them. "Got far to walk have you?"

Periwinkle stopped and introduced himself and told the men that he was an explorer and was on his way to Egypt and from there to other lands that hadn't yet been discovered … wherever they might be.

"To Egypt?" queried the man who had first called to him. "How are you going to get there?"

"I will probably walk for most of the way," answered Periwinkle. "I would very much like to find a train or a bus or a lift in a car for some of the journey though. I've done rather a lot of walking so far."

To tell the truth, Periwinkle was starting to feel a bit fed up of walking. He wasn't entirely displeased when the man told him that he couldn't possibly walk to Egypt. It was too far and too dangerous.

He was less pleased with the way that the conversation went next. It appeared that he had been misled about it being easy to get from Greece to Egypt: There were no trains. There wasn't a bus service. The café men were fairly certain that he wouldn't find anyone who would drive there in a car. The only way that Periwinkle could get to Egypt from Greece would be by boat. This wasn't what he wanted to hear.

Feeling somewhat downhearted, Periwinkle thanked the men for their advice and set off once more. It was getting late and he needed to find somewhere to spend the night.

Not far out of the village he found a patch of grass underneath a hedge by the side of the lane. It looked comfortable enough so Periwinkle sat down. He nibbled a couple of biscuits and tried not to think too much about what the café men had told him. He was sure it would seem less of a problem after a good night's sleep.

The next morning dawned cloudy. The sun was reluctant to make an appearance so the sky was grey which mirrored Periwinkle's mood. Despite sleeping well, he now had to face the problem of how to continue his journey.

He ate some breakfast and thought for a while. He was in no hurry to set off again. He'd rather lost his appetite for exploring Greece.

Eventually he decided that he should at least start walking to somewhere, even if he wasn't entirely sure where that somewhere might be or which direction it might be in. He was busy thinking a lot about how he was going to continue his journey and not very much about where he was or what he was doing. Determined to get on his way he stepped out from under the hedge and onto the lane.

He was jerked back to reality by the dreadful noise of squealing brakes and he looked up to see a lorry hurtling towards him. He jumped back under the hedge with his heart pounding so hard that he thought it might jump right out of his chest.

The lorry came to a halt and a very red-faced driver jumped out of it, waving his arms around. "What do you think you're doing?" he shouted. "Gave me a proper shock seeing you there. Why did you step out in front of me you silly piglet?"

Periwinkle thought the man might have been a bit more apologetic about nearly running him over. But in fairness it had been his – Periwinkle's – fault. He realised, a little late, that it is very sensible when you're near a road, or even a lane, to think about traffic and not about other things. He resolved that in future he would concentrate on roads when he was near one. If he needed to think hard about other things he would do it when he was sitting down safely.

On top of his fed-upness and not knowing how he was going to continue his journey to Egypt it was all a bit too much for Periwinkle. He no longer felt like a brave explorer and adventurer. He did the only thing possible in the circumstances and burst into tears!

The lorry driver stopped shouting and waving his arms around.

"Don't cry piglet. I know I was cross with you but I didn't want to make you cry. No harm done eh? We're both safe." He gave Periwinkle a red handkerchief which Periwinkle used to wipe the tears from his face. He explained that he was Periwinkle Pig, Explorer and he was fed up because he had managed to get all the way from England to Greece but now he didn't know how to get to Egypt which was where he really really wanted to get to.

"And I'm very sorry I stepped out in front of you," he finished.

"I think I can help you there Periwinkle," said the lorry driver. "As it happens I'm on my way to Egypt and I'm happy for you to come with me. You'll be good company."

Well, this was excellent news. Periwinkle could go to Egypt in a lorry!

"Are you really driving all the way there?" he asked.

The lorry driver laughed. "Oh no, it's too far and too dangerous. I'm going by boat. It only takes a couple of days."

Periwinkle started to get sad again and told the

lorry driver about the boat and the storm and falling into the sea on the lid of a packing case.

"That must have been a small boat," suggested the lorry driver. "The one I'm going on is a very big boat. In fact it's not really a boat at all. It's more of a cargo ship. A sort of ferry for lorries."

Periwinkle brightened up again. This sounded much better and, if he'd understood correctly, he could be in Egypt in a couple of days' time which was an exciting thought for a piglet who had been so fed up just a little while earlier.

The lorry driver introduced himself as Leon and held out his hand which Periwinkle shook.

"Come on then Periwinkle. Jump in. We'd best be on our way else we'll miss the sailing."

Periwinkle climbed up into the lorry. Leon climbed up too and he began to drive the lorry towards a big boat that would take them to Egypt.

Periwinkle listens to some sailors

Periwinkle had never travelled in a lorry before and now he was in Leon's lorry on his way to catch a boat that would take him to Egypt. He was amazed to find how high above the ground he was in the front of the lorry and how much he could see from up there.

As they travelled they talked. Periwinkle told Leon about his journeying and adventures. Leon told Periwinkle about some of the places he'd been to in his lorry. Periwinkle thought it sounded very interesting and he was reassured that Leon had been on lots of boats and hadn't fallen off any of them even when there had been a storm.

After a few hours they reached the sea which was shining brightly in the sunshine that had at last made an appearance.

"There's our boat Periwinkle," announced Leon, pointing at something that Periwinkle wouldn't even have realised was a boat. He had been promised a very big boat and this certainly was. It was as big as a building. A very big building. It towered above them as they drove up next to it.

Periwinkle breathed a sigh of relief. He was sure this boat would sail through any storms without a problem. He briefly wondered how something so big could float but he pushed that thought as far back in his mind as he could possibly get it. He didn't need to know how it did it; he just had to believe that it would.

A tall man in a white uniform and wearing a peaked cap walked up to their lorry. Leon wound down the window and handed him some papers. The uniform looked at the papers, made a thumbs-up sign and waved them forward onto the boat.

Leon parked his lorry next to other lorries and switched off the engine. He explained to Periwinkle that he was going to sleep in a room but, although it was a very big boat, it would be a very small room and there wouldn't be space for Periwinkle to sleep there too.

"But you can sleep here on the front seat," he offered. "You can look after the lorry and make sure nobody steals anything from it. If anybody asks, tell them that you're a guard-piglet! See you in Egypt Periwinkle!"

It had been a long day and it was getting late. Periwinkle ate a few biscuits and then settled down on the front seat of the lorry. He was fast asleep by the time the boat set sail.

The following morning Periwinkle stretched his arms and legs and, having run out of acorns, he had a few more of his dwindling supply of biscuits and then set off from the lorry to have a look around. He was sure there would be a lot for an exploring piglet to discover on such a big boat.

He opened a door and found himself out in the fresh air. Ahead of him he could see nothing but sea. He stood and looked at it for a while, marvelling at how much of it there was. It looked much less frightening when you were high above it on a very big boat and not on the lid of a packing case that had fallen off a much smaller boat. He couldn't even feel the boat moving and he was pleased to find that it wasn't bobbing up and down and making his tummy feel strange.

So engrossed was he in looking at the sea that he hadn't noticed he was no longer on his own until a coughing noise worked its way through his ears to his brain. He looked around and saw that he was being observed by a pair of large green eyes.

He was surprised to see a cat on a boat. He wasn't sure why he was surprised. After all, some people might have been surprised to see a piglet on a boat but here he was.

It looked like a well-travelled cat. Its fur was uneven, with large chunks missing. One ear stuck up in the air but the other hung down and didn't seem to be complete. Its tail appeared to have had some inches chopped off it. It spoke with a rough voice rather than the soft purring sort of voice that cats usually have.

"Who might you be?" it demanded.

"I am Periwinkle Pig and I am an explorer. I am on my way to Egypt and then to other lands …"

"That's as maybe," he was interrupted. "Have you been to Turkey?"

Periwinkle had to admit that he had not. Nor, he had to admit in response to further questions, had he been to Cyprus, to Israel and, of course, not yet to Egypt.

"Strikes me you've not done a lot of exploring at all," sneered the cat.

"I'm only just starting to be an explorer," Periwinkle defended himself. "I have already come a long way from England and had lots of adventures on my way. But I'm always willing to learn from another explorer, particularly one so well-travelled as you seem to be."

"I'm not an explorer," stated the cat. "I'm a sailor. A very experienced sailor I would add. I've been to lots of countries," he went on and proceeded to tell Periwinkle about his travels. "I sail around Greece and Egypt. Sometimes I go to Turkey. Occasionally Italy if I have to. I don't actually get off the boat you understand. But oh yes, I've been all over."

It seemed to Periwinkle that the cat hadn't been to very many places at all.

"Have you been to England?" he enquired.

The cat looked thoughtful. "Not sure I have. Is it nice and warm there?"

Periwinkle said that, whilst it was very nice in England, there were times that it wasn't warm at all.

"Can't see the point in going anywhere that isn't warm," stated the cat. "I'm not one for cold. I don't think that England would suit me at all so I don't think I'll bother going."

Periwinkle was getting a bit tired of the cat's conversation which didn't seem very interesting. Not like his own conversation of course.

"Who's sailing this boat whilst you're out here talking to me?" he asked. The cat told him that, although he was in charge of the boat, there were some human sailors who steered it and made sure that they didn't sail into any rocks or bits of land.

"Here are a couple of them now," he finished, pointing with one tatty paw at two men walking towards them. The men were wearing blue trousers and t-shirts with blue and white stripes across them. One had white hair and a bushy white beard which made him look as though his face was surrounded by a ring of white fur. The other man had no hair at all, just a very shiny head.

"Sinbad been boring you about being a sailor has he?" asked the bushy-face as the two men got closer.

"You should talk to proper sailors like us," added the shiny-head. "We could tell you a few stories."

"I would be very interested to hear them," replied Periwinkle. "For I am an explorer myself and I like to hear about travelling and adventures."

Sinbad the cat tutted and, with a muttered "Real sailors eh? What do they know?", he stalked away with his ragged tail waving furiously.

The two sailors sat down and began to tell their stories. Periwinkle sat with them and listened and he found what they had to say absolutely fascinating.

He sat with them and listened to their stories the next day and the day after that too. Then the bushy-face told Periwinkle that they wouldn't be able to tell him any more stories because the boat would be arriving in Egypt the following morning. This made Periwinkle very excited but not too excited to remember his manners so he thanked them for their company and went back to Leon's lorry where he settled down for the night. It was still early but when you're excited about something happening the next day it is a good idea to go to bed early.

He fell asleep with a smile on his face, knowing that when he woke up he would be in Egypt.

Periwinkle pushes a car

Periwinkle was having difficulty persuading his eyes to open but he came wide awake as Leon, the lorry driver, climbed back into the driver's seat with a cheery greeting.

"We're here Periwinkle! I told you this boat would get you safely to Egypt didn't I?"

Periwinkle sat up quickly. He'd been a bit afraid that he'd just been dreaming and he wasn't anywhere near Egypt at all. But Leon sounded very real and very certain.

Suddenly the massive door in front of all the lorries opened and everything was bathed in bright sunshine. Egyptian sunshine!

The lorries began to move and Leon drove off the very big boat that had got them safely to Egypt. A short distance from the boat he stopped the lorry.

"This is as far as I can take you Periwinkle. I'm just going to unload the lorry and then I'll be heading back to Greece on the next boat."

Periwinkle had hoped that Leon might be driving all the way to the Pyramids. He'd enjoyed riding in the lorry high above the ground. But he thanked Leon for getting him safely to Egypt, climbed down from the lorry and waved as Leon drove away.

He looked around him and saw a road leading away from the coast. He didn't know where it led to but that didn't make much difference. Anywhere away from the coast was going to be more or less south and that was the general direction that Periwinkle knew he must follow. He hitched his duffel bag onto his shoulder and set off in that direction.

In Europe Periwinkle had walked along lanes and roads that didn't look too different to the ones he'd walked along in England. He'd gone through towns and villages that looked very similar to English towns and villages.

Egypt was different. There weren't any country lanes; just a road that was very straight and stretched a long way into the distance. Instead of hedges and fields, the road had sand at either side for as far as Periwinkle could see. There weren't any villages; there were no shops or churches or cosy-looking cafes with happy people outside. There were no friendly farmers or cosy barns where he could spend the night.

Occasionally he came across something that, at one time, might have been a building but had fallen down and was now not much more than a pile of stones.

For most of the time he walked along the road and at night he slept in the sand which made a comfortable enough resting place even if it did get into his clothes and needed to be shaken out in the morning before he could set off again.

One morning Periwinkle found that he was being followed by a thin dog with a small head and a very sharply-pointed nose. For days he had been on his own and was keen to have someone to talk to for a while so he stopped to give the dog chance to catch up with him.

"Hello Mr Dog," he greeted him. "I am Periwinkle Pig, Explorer. We appear to be going in the same direction so perhaps we might walk together for a while?"

He was a bit taken aback when the dog said firmly "I might look like a dog but I'm a wild animal you know. Oh yes, I'm a wild animal. I go where I want. Do what I want. I answer to no-one. Explorer are you? You're not doing much exploring just standing here so you'd better get on your way. I'll walk with you for a bit if you insist."

The two of them walked along together talking of this and that. After a while they came across two horses. Like the dog they were thin and their coats were dusty from the sand which was thrown up as they cantered across it.

"What are a piglet and a dog doing walking together along this road?" asked one of them.

"What is a piglet doing in Egypt at all?" asked the other.

So Periwinkle introduced himself and explained that he was on his way to see the Pyramids and that he'd met up with the dog and they were walking together for a while.

The horses said that they would walk with them too.

Now there were four of them walking along and talking. They hadn't noticed a bright red car coming up from behind until it tooted its horn and its engine roared as it passed them. It was driving along very very quickly.

"Not sure what all the hurry is," grumbled the dog and the horses agreed.

They continued to walk and talk and a little further along they came across the red car again. It had gone off the side of the road and was now stuck in the sand. The driver was sitting in the car trying to make it move but the wheels were just spinning round and round and the car was getting more and more stuck.

When he saw them, the driver jumped out of the car. He explained that he'd had to swerve to avoid a snake on the road and the car had ended up in the sand. He wondered if the animals could help him.

The dog and the horses didn't look as though they wanted to help.

"No snakes here," said the dog. "You were just going too fast."

"Your own silly fault," added one of the horses. "You should be more careful."

"Come on, let's see what we can do," Periwinkle suggested to the animals in what he hoped was a persuasive tone of voice.

"I don't suppose you've got a strong rope in your car?" he asked the driver who replied that, unfortunately, he hadn't thought to pack one. Periwinkle looked around him as though hoping that a rope shop would suddenly materialise but of course it didn't.

As he wondered what else to suggest he noticed the dog had walked off down the road in the direction from which they had come and was now coming back towards them carrying something in his mouth.

"Here's your snake," he muttered as he dropped his treasure onto the ground in front of the driver. "It's a rope, not a snake … which you'd have realised if you hadn't been driving so fast. Now, what did you want a rope for Periwinkle?"

Periwinkle had no idea where the rope had come from. He guessed it had probably fallen off one of the lorries that had passed him earlier. But he didn't mind how it had arrived. It was just convenient that it had. He attached the rope to the front of the car and, not without difficulty, persuaded the two horses to pull on it whilst he, the dog and the driver pushed from the back.

It took a lot of effort and the dog kept moaning and the horses occasionally dropped the rope because they were complaining too, but at last they managed to get the car back onto the road.

The driver whistled in relief.

"Thank goodness you all came along when you did. I thought I was going to be stuck here. Now, I must be on my way. Can I offer any of you a lift?" he asked.

"Not likely," said the dog. "I've no wish to go so fast."

"Certainly not," added the horses.

Periwinkle had enjoyed the company of the dog and the horses but he'd had enough of walking on a road with nothing but sand at either side. "Are you going anywhere near the Pyramids?" he asked hopefully. The answer brought a smile to his face.

"The Pyramids? Yes, that's exactly where I'm going! Well, almost. Near enough anyway."

Periwinkle had often found on his journeying that, when he did a good turn for someone, he was given a good turn back and so it was on this occasion.

"In which case I will happily accept a lift in your rather smart car," he thanked the driver.

After saying goodbye to the dog and the horses who tutted and muttered and said things like "rather you than us" Periwinkle got into the bright red car which sped away along the very straight road in the direction of the Pyramids.

Periwinkle is impressed by the Pyramids

Periwinkle had reached Egypt and, right now, was in a bright red car which was taking him towards the Pyramids. The car was travelling faster than Periwinkle was entirely happy with but he was trying not to think too much about that.

The car driver chattered away as he drove but, unusually, Periwinkle didn't add much to the conversation and, in fact, was barely listening to what the driver had to say. He found himself preoccupied with the scenery and was fascinated by how it changed as the miles passed. Since being in Egypt he had seen a lot of sand, very few buildings, even fewer trees and no green fields at all. As they sped along Periwinkle started to see collections of buildings that almost looked like villages. There were cows in fields. At one point they crossed over a wide river which had large boats on it.

From time to time they passed signposts pointing reassuringly to the Pyramids in the exact direction in which they were travelling.

Eventually, and to Periwinkle's relief, the bright red car had to slow down. They had reached a place where there were a lot more buildings. There were people and animals walking in the road and a huge amount of traffic. It seemed to Periwinkle that all the cars and vans and bicycles in Egypt must be in this very place.

He concluded that they must be somewhere important. He had only just started thinking about what that might mean when the bright red car came to a stop in front of a building. A sign on it said that it was a hotel. More excitingly it was 'The Pyramid Hotel'.

"Here we are then!" announced the driver of the bright red car. "It's not actually the Pyramids but they're not far away. Sort of … over there," and he waved one hand in some general direction that Periwinkle couldn't totally follow. "Thanks again for sorting me out after I'd seen that snake. You don't talk much do you? I never found out why a piglet was trying to get to the Pyramids but here we are anyway."

Periwinkle felt it was a bit late to explain about being an explorer and that he'd set off from his home in England to get to Egypt and see the Pyramids before going on to places that haven't yet been discovered. It would take him a lot of time and he had more important things to do so he thanked the driver for bringing him to the Pyramids and got out of the bright red car.

He sensed that his little compass wasn't going to be too much help in finding the Pyramids 'over there' but, fortunately, just nearby was another helpful signpost which pointed to 'over there'. He hitched his duffel bag back onto his shoulder and followed the arrow on the signpost.

Periwinkle had thought that Paris was busy and noisy but this was even busier and even noisier. It was hard to walk along the pavement as there were so many people already walking on it and it seemed to Periwinkle that most of them were walking towards him. Sometimes he was forced to stop and let them pass him.

He walked and walked. It was further than he was expecting. It was a very hot day. The sky was hazy and everything was dusty and sandy. Periwinkle was just thinking that he would find somewhere to stop for a rest and perhaps one of his remaining sandwiches when, through the haze, he thought he could just about make out what looked like a large triangle pointing up into the sky.

He blinked and shook his head. He wondered whether the heat was making his mind play tricks. He looked again. It was definitely a triangle. Forgetting that, just a few moments ago, he had wanted to stop for a break and refreshments, he walked on.

The triangle got bigger and, before too long he could see another, smaller, triangle. And then the road he was on opened out and they were right in front of him. The Pyramids!

"Wow!" he breathed. And then, again, "Wow!"

Periwinkle had seen pictures of the Pyramids in his books but all the pictures in the world couldn't prepare him for actually being there and seeing them for himself. They were much larger than he'd imagined. He had always known that sometimes it is better to see something yourself if you can rather than just look at a picture. It was why it was such a wonderful thing to be an explorer.

To Periwinkle's delight he found that he could walk right up to the biggest of the Pyramids and even touch it. He walked around it. It took him a long time as there were four sides and each of them was twice the length of the football pitch that he'd run up and down when he'd been a football mascot. Each side was shaped like a triangle and the four triangles sort of leaned together and met at a point high up in the sky.

Periwinkle knew that they were made of blocks of stone but it was only when he got close up that he realised just how huge the stones were. Each one of them was taller than him and they looked extremely heavy. He also knew that the Pyramids had been built a very long time ago and he wondered how it had been done. The stones were surely too big and too heavy for even a hundred people to have moved them and built them up so high. It was a bit of a mystery.

There was another famous thing that Periwinkle wanted to see and, luckily, there was another of those useful signposts pointing the way to it. He touched the Pyramid one more time and then set off on his way.

Not too much further down the road he found what he was looking for; a giant statue called the Sphinx. It was a strange statue in Periwinkle's opinion. He'd seen plenty of statues of people and many statues of animals but this was a bit of both. It had the face of a man but the body of an animal. Perhaps a lion. Maybe a dog. Periwinkle was sure it wasn't a pig. A notice close-by told him that it had been built to guard the Pyramids. Periwinkle wasn't sure who or what it was guarding them from but, as they were still standing after all these lots and lots of years, he thought it must be doing a reasonable job.

He stood and looked again at the strange statue and at the great Pyramid not too far behind it. It made him feel a bit strange and he found a little tear forming in his eye. Not a sad tear but the sort that we all get sometimes when something lovely has happened.

What a day it had been. Which reminded Periwinkle that it had also been a long day and now, perhaps, it was time to find somewhere to spend the night.

Periwinkle makes a big decision

So here we find Periwinkle next to the strange part-man, part-animal statue called the Sphinx which was guarding the triangular buildings called pyramids.

He was starting to feel hungry as it was a long time since he'd last eaten so his next task was to find somewhere comfortable to settle to eat and sleep. He looked around him to find a spot that would be suitable.

As he looked he noticed a group of camels plodding towards him.

"Hello little piglet," one greeted him as they approached.

"You can take a photo of us if you want," said a second. "Lots of people take photos of us."

Periwinkle was about to explain that he didn't have a camera when a third camel joined in the conversation. "Hope you're not wanting a ride to the Pyramids. We've finished work for the day. If you want a ride you'll have to wait until tomorrow."

Periwinkle assured the camels that he wasn't looking for a ride. If he was, he thought, then it wouldn't be on the back of a camel which looked a dangerous thing to do. He'd had his share of danger for today after being driven very fast in the bright red car that had brought him (almost) to the Pyramids.

"No, I am not looking for a ride. In fact I am beginning to look for somewhere that I might spend the night. Would you know of anywhere?"

The camels talked a little amongst themselves mumbling in such a way that Periwinkle couldn't make out what they were saying. Eventually one of them turned to him.

"You could come home with us if you want? We've got plenty of hay and don't mind sharing it with you."

"Provided you don't snore," added one of the others.

Periwinkle didn't know whether he snored or not. He wasn't sure how anybody knew whether they snored because you only snore when you're asleep and, if you're asleep, then you can't hear yourself snore can you? It was another of those mysteries. Not as much a mystery as how the Pyramids had been built of course but then not all mysteries have to be big ones.

He was pleased to accept their offer of a bed for the night and walked along with them as they headed home. They wanted to know what a piglet was doing in Egypt so he told them about his journeying and how excited he was to finally see the Pyramids.

He wondered whether the camels knew how the Pyramids had been built but they had no idea.

"They were here when I got here," said one.

"I think they've always been here," added a second.

"Never thought about it," drawled a third.

They all sounded rather disinterested and Periwinkle supposed that was because they weren't explorers. Explorers always want to know things.

When they got to where the camels lived they showed him a patch of hay where he could sleep. The camels made themselves some supper from grass and leaves which they'd hidden underneath another patch of hay before they'd gone to work that morning.

Periwinkle took out a sandwich from his duffel bag, concerned to see that it was the last one in there. He ate it very slowly, trying to make it last as long as he possibly could.

He and the camels sat talking long into the evening. Periwinkle told them about his journeying and the adventures he'd had. Suddenly a memory popped right into the front of his mind.

"Do you dance?" he asked. The camels looked at him as though he'd asked the most stupid question in the entire world. "Dance? Camels don't dance. We've got too many legs for it. They just get tangled up with each other if we try to dance. You've got the same number of legs as us. Do you dance?"

Periwinkle said that no, he didn't dance but had met two camels that did. "Well, I suppose it was a sort of dancing," he added, remembering their slightly awkward movement. He told the story of the circus in England where he'd met two camels who had come from Egypt and lived near the Pyramids.

One of the older camels thought for a moment.

"Do you mean Colin and Clarence? I remember them. Always moaning about the sand and the heat and the flies. Always showing off too. In a circus now are they? In England? I don't suppose there are many camels in England. Not our sort of weather from what I understand."

Eventually the camels said it was time they turned in for the night. "We have to work tomorrow so we can't sit up all night chatting to you, interesting though you are".

Periwinkle settled himself down in the hay and shut his eyes. "I got here!" he said to himself as he began to drift off to sleep. "I truly am an explorer."

Several hours later Periwinkle awoke and found that the camels had already gone to work and the sun was doing a splendid job of lighting up the Pyramids.

He sat up and realised that he now had to face a question that he had been putting off. It was the question that the wine farmer had asked when he was in France; how would he know when he'd found somewhere that nobody else had found?

He had a new question too; until now he had been focussed on getting to Egypt but which way should he go from here? He wondered whether all explorers had faced similar questions and, if they had, from where did they find their answers?

It was time for Periwinkle to do some hard thinking. He always found thinking easier when he had a full tummy so he reached into his duffel bag to find something for breakfast. The sandwiches that his mother had packed for him had finally run out. He appeared to be in a part of the world where there were no acorns. He still had some biscuits left though so he nibbled a couple of those and sat and tried to decide what to do.

The food situation troubled him. He couldn't just keep eating biscuits. Besides, he was rather missing his mother's cooking. In fact, now he came to think of it, he was rather missing his mother. And his friends. And his Auntie Pink.

He hoped his mother had received copies of all the photographs that had been taken of him and all the newspapers that his picture had been in. He knew she would be very proud of him but perhaps she was missing him too.

He wasn't sure how long he'd been away from home but it felt like a very long time since he'd told his mother he was going to go travelling. He'd become an explorer and had managed to explore as far as Egypt which was a big achievement for a little piglet.

He wondered whether, without realising it, he might already have discovered places that nobody had discovered before. He had walked through lots of places where there was absolutely nobody there. He was a bit annoyed with himself that he couldn't remember exactly where they were so that he could tell people about them.

It didn't mean he was any less of an explorer because he hadn't had a small country named after him. He thought he could reasonably call himself an adventurer as he'd had so many adventures along the way. He'd met some very interesting people and creatures.

It was going to take a long time to tell his family and friends all about it.

These thoughts were all leading him to one conclusion.

"I will set off for home," he determined. "I'm sure that all the great explorers went home sometimes.

I can always go exploring again. There's still a lot of world that I haven't seen and my mother will be able to make me another supply of sandwiches.

"Yes, I will definitely go home for a while."

That was a very big decision for a little piglet. He nibbled on another biscuit, looked around him at Egypt and smiled the biggest smile he'd ever smiled.

"Now," he said to himself. "All I have to do is work out how to get home. And I wonder what adventures I might have along the way?"

THE END
(or is it?)

Also by Peter Cutler & Kath Kyle,

"The Adventures of Periwinkle Pig"

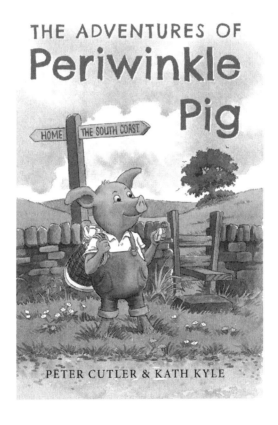

THE ADVENTURES OF
Periwinkle
Pig

HOME | THE SOUTH COAST

PETER CUTLER & KATH KYLE